# CAMP BASAWA

WANel

# Camp Basawa

Other titles by WANel

Incomplete
Kafrika
Miss Abishag Gets Married
PTSD
Breastfeeding
Voyage
Camp Basawa
One week last summer
My Brother My Lover, Where art thou
A Drunken Lion and Three Warthogs around a New Year's Eve
Desert Fire
Mother & Son Reunion
Frikkie Volume 1
Die Vrolike Homoseksueel

Enjoy!

# Arrival!

A single gate allowed the only access to Camp Basawa.

By the time we arrived the sun began to sink behind the dune walls. Evening crept over the series of terraced sand dunes. The sand dunes rose and fell like waves on an ocean - not that I have ever seen the sea before I landed inside Camp Basawa.

A narrow dusty road lead up to the gate. A ten foot high alarmed barbed wire fence enclosed the camp. Inside and outside the fence grinning skulled signed yellow plate warned trespassers.

☠ Mind the land man fields
Guaranteed express departure to hell ☠

Above the skulled signs a single finger pointed at a stairway to heaven for the stupidly brave enough to wander beyond the grinning skulls.

Oh boy, someone sure had a sense of humour, sickly so. I was under no illusion that in all probability I'd get myself killed with the first few days of arrival.

Through the dirt smeared windows I gazed at this picture of mighty desolation. Without sniffing the outside air I sensed the desolation loneliness clouding scattered buildings and tents. Inside the fence there was nothing more red brick buildings build in a U-shape.

Inside the U a scattering of tents erected.

At the top of the right hand side of the U stood a lonely little house. The ground in front of it cleared. A flag pole with no flag hoist stood forlorn. Under a scattering of thorn trees stood another tent with its flaps rolled up.

I remember from somewhere over a dune snaked what looked like a water pipe. The pipe ran into the camp and up to a rusty water-tank sat on top of a wooden tower.

At the entrance stood another watch tower.

Oh boy I thought by myself, this is a place one can die and within a matter of days be nothing more than a clean scavenged corpse.

I looked around.

The bus rattled through the gates and came to a halt at the side of the cleared piece of land in the middle of the desert. Not another living soul was in sight.

Since we departed from the school grounds earlier in the morning we had no contact without another human. The two sergeants accompanying us prohibited conversation. Inside the fence there was nothing more than a single row of red brick buildings and ten randomly pitched brown military tents.

I spotted a forlorn looking flag pole with no flag hanging from it. It stood in the middle of a cleared piece of land.

From somewhere over a dune what looked like a water pipe, snaked into the camp and ran up to a water-tank on top of a wooden tower.

A guard tower

We slept in asbestos barracks on thin horsehair mattress with a single sheet and paper-thin blanket. Nasty blankets. Lectures, church services and medical examinations took place in camouflaged tents.

The tent sides rolled up in a desperate attempt to attract a breeze while temperatures under the canvas roofs soared. The barracks were furnaces in the summer, and in winter our rooms turned into slaughterhouses fridges.

A single row of red brick buildings housed the scientists, people seldom seen, with rooms at the back of the buildings, they left camp by helicopter, permission for us to visit was limited to psychological observation periods.

Abel and I were separated soon after we stepped from the bus. The sun, a fierce ball of fire, set behind the dunes, creating a spectacular end to the day, the only thing of beauty upon our arrival.

Disorientated, hungry, tired and a long way from home comforts. I was not even sure why I stood where I stood and why I was not on my bed listening to the radio and the latest pop songs. The sergeant and corporals lined us up into a single row.

From one of the tents ten officers in combat clothes

appeared. Their shoulders carried the weight of their ranks. Men with grim faces, two younger officers carried the files. The despicable General stepped forward. There was no bloody escape from the man.

'I am General Venter. From this moment I am your Commander. Your life is mine. You are not my children, yet, but I will make you mine. I am your Father for all intents and purpose. I represent the will of the State and God. You will obey me and my men, until such time as you deserve our trust. Look around you,' he stopped for a theatrical pause, I did'n react much, I sensed from this point onwards it would best to keep what you think to yourself, 'there is nowhere to run from here, but death. And death you will meet out there, the sun will bleach your bones alongside the whales, seal and elephants, creatures tougher than any one of you, not even they could survive.'

The man made his point.

One by one a file was handed to the General. The day darkened and the last rays faded. A shiver ran down my spine. I never saw such an inhospitable piece of land. They read our names, one by one.

The General paged through the file, then scrutinised the mostly scrawny things in front of him. My brother was the only fit boy. With a pointed hand the General ordered the boys left or right. Abel and I remained standing alone.

The General read our names and we stepped forward. His pale blue killer eyes penetrated our souls.

I tried to hold his gaze but failed miserably. I backed down within less than a minute. The man unsettled me big time, such brutal masculine magnetism, I felt overpowered.

He stepped forward. His right hand thumb pushed my head up, the left hand the face of Abel.

Intensely he studied our faces, turned them left and right like a horse buyer making a purchase.

I was convinced any moment the General would asked me to show my teeth. To my surprise his touch was cool on my warm skin. He smelled nice, fresh shower soap. What was wrong with me, I felt a strange attraction for this man.

'Well, well, well,' he said, 'the Du Preez brothers, at last I make your acquaintance.'

The man was such a liar!

'Welcome to Camp Basawa gentlemen. Your grandfather was a great man.'

He knew Grandpa Jack? What the bloody heckle?

'Don't disappoint him or his legacy, I shall keep my eye on you two.'

His voice dropped to a whisper. It was then I just knew, I could never lie to this man. He waved Abel to the right, I joined the two boys on the left. A cold shudder ran down my spine, despite the late afternoon desert heat. No! This was not possible. Murder, horror! Fried green tomatoes. Separated from my brother in this desolate environment. Doomed to spending the night with strangers. Oh horror of all horrors. I looked into the fierce eyes of Sergeant snake. The blood drained from my face. A malicious smile spread over his face. He marched us off, Abel disappeared in the opposite direction. Winter descended in my life. My lover not by my side. Oh how will I survive, slowly the fire died inside of me. Life in Camp Basawa was not going to taste like champagne.

Thirteen boys awaited our arrival in the pink painted barracks. The pale moon shone on their faces. I saw the look in their eyes as they looked into mine.

They said not a word, but I understood their body language. They sat on beds lining both sides of the building, but jumped to attention as the sergeant entered. I decide to say nothing. By my estimation we were the same age.

I scanned the room. The boys were all very pretty. What was I doing here.

Their heads shaved. I felt the same uneasy feeling when in the history classroom Miss Myburgh showed us concentration camp newsreels.

'Ladies, I shall leave you to it,' Sergeant said and walked off.

I chose a bed. At the end of each bed stood a tin chest. In the chests our uniforms, black camouflage pants and T-shirts. A washing bag with toiletries awaited our arrival.

We arrived with empty hands, not even a book or a photo was permitted. Just us, our bodies and our minds entered the camp. The boys on either side introduced themselves as Marius and Johan.

As I was in no mood to make conversation they soon returned to their beds. I trusted no one. I decided to maintain this strategy until I sussed the true nature of this camp. A heavenly decision. Half an hour later it was lights out.

No supper served.

Bastards!

No watches permitted.

The thought of what was permitted filled me with

dread. Did I head for an early grave, either under the boot of Sergeant Snake, electrocuted by the fence, or eaten alive by the desert and it's ferocious inhabitants.

I did not sleep much on my first night. I stared at the ceiling and watched Marius and Andre in their sleep. Their chests heaved gently, Marius was a light snorer.

I wondered if Abel was awake, thinking of me. I remained doubtful. My thoughts travelled south across the lands we drove through into the house where our mother slept alone. I drew comfort for inside her was another sibling growing. She was not alone completely. Did she pace the house tonight, was she scared?

Sometime during the night, the barrack door creaked open. The bulk figure of the Sergeant filled the door. I veiled my eyes as he moved up the walkway inspecting the contents of the beds. At my bed he stopped.

Bloody quickly I shut my eyes tight. I smelled him, sensed him, slowed my breathing down, fending off the hatred I felt for this ugly man from seeping through my pores, the man with sly eyes, like a cold-blooded snake. Tonight for sure was not Xmas night, despite the chill in my heart.

'What do you want from me,' I dared whisperingly ask into a finite dark space.

'You will soon enough find out, then I will tear you up, scatter your tissue pieces into a desert grave.'

His footfall disappeared.

I opened my eyes and spit hate and fear in equal measure in the direction of his back, the chambers of my heart cold inside from this man's audacious insults.

'When I speak of our enemies, I refer to our natural enemies. The ones trying to steal this land from us, the

land won in battles our forefathers fought . The
ownership of the land signed over in blood of men killed
defending their women, children who had nowhere to
go. When you kill, you kill with dedication and a passion
for the cause. You always kill first. You do not think. You
do not hesitate. You apply your training skills with
dedication. Killing is about survival. Life is about
survival. Kill or be killed.'

His words sunk in as he looked over the army of
shaved heads. His eyes looked strained. We did not
move.

We sat bloody still.

The weather was dull, just like winter in London. You
did not swat the fly on your nose. You did not stop the
rolling sweat beads. Your soon to be become killer hands
clasped together, motionless on your lap. The pale blue
eyes hypnotised each boy. It was utterly ridiculous.

'You stab before you are stabbed or even worse,
stabbed in the back, for they, who are as dark as the
night, prowl like hungry panthers on the lookout for
easy prey. Do not leave your sides unguarded, they circle
around us like hyenas, driven by a cowardly hunger to
sweep us from this land. Be a hunter, be a predator and
kill swiftly and quietly. Do not boast about your killings,
for life does not take kindly to losing one of its own. The
boy with the slow hands will be the best.'

Morning lectures were delivered in the tents. Any
address by General Venter caused great excitement and
anticipation within me. A man of knowledge and infinite
wisdom, a compassionate speaker, believing in the cause,
his manner with the boys was firm and relaxed.

We attended his lectures after breakfast. In the first
few weeks I found it hard going. Sitting still, focusing

when sleep sidestepped me in the night, despite the rigorous physical regime we endured at Camp Basawa.

Easy it was not.

Each morning we rose at four, with the exception of Sundays. First activity of the day was a 2.4 kilometre run along a dusty road outside the camp.

The boys of each barrack ran as a platoon with their sergeant in front of them. We sang whilst running. The sergeants rap-sang the lyrics, we repeated. It was bloody fantastic. I sang my lungs out, top of my voice.

Chorus girl, chorus girl, just like my dear friend Nana-Noo many years later on a camp site near Dorset. The songs were epic poems about warriors setting off to distant lands leaving their beloved countries behind.

The booming voices of the sergeants travelled over the plains and ours followed. When your platoon ran in silence, you listened to the singing of the boys in front or behind with a sense of pride welling up, a sense of belonging, strangers thrown together, singing of their melancholic longing for the comfort of a mother, a mother who gave you away.

After a while the distance did not matter, you ran transfixed by the singing in this no mans land that slowly worked its magic and as the days sped by I developed a passion for the barrenness of the land. The nothingness of the land reflected the soul stripped of feelings.

The barrenness of the land was deceiving, it was rich in wild life. Species adapted to the inhospitable world they inhabited, large and small, herds of springbok, gemsbok and ostriches roamed the land, stopped grazing when we ran pass them.

The dune dwellings crawled with insects and reptiles.

The occasional lonely lion could be seen dragging a seal, killed in its sleep, across the dunes. When sleep evaded me in the darkest hours of the night I drew comfort from the roar of a lion, somewhere out there in the dunes, on the prowl, searching for a prey, waiting to kill.

Abel and I saw each other from a distance.

He encouraged me with a wink.

My brother became a distant figure in my life, the few hours camp life allowed us together became jewels I treasured when it was time for us to be together. Our lectures and practical training never overlapped.

We took our meals at separate tables. The reason for our separation remained unclear, whether it had something to do with the interviews we endured in the days after our arrival, I do not know.

Despite our brotherly closeness, we were creatures of opposite natures.

Like the sun and the moon we complimented each other from opposite ends of the galaxies we moved in.

To my relief, Sergeant Snake, I never called him by his real name, not in life, nor in my imagination, was only assigned as our herder, keeping us together, shepherding us to the next activity, once inside the classroom he kept a distance and a watchful eye on us, hovering like a vulture awaiting its turn at taking a bite at the spoils. In our case, this was the two hours physical training at the end of each day.

Gorgeous looking Lieutenant Herholdt was assigned to look after our wellbeing, our guardian, mentor, the shoulder to cry on, not that one dared, without good cause, crying was frowned on, an intolerable male activity, a sign of weakness and in the words of General

Venter, 'a man permitting tears from his eyes, would betray his mother in the hour of need.

Lieutenant Herholdt had a slow hand.

He looked like Tom Cruise. Oh so macho he was.

I had the hots from the first moment my eyes fell on him. A man of a fine swimmer's physique he was, our lieutenant Herholdt. He had perfect white teeth that he frequently displayed when he threw back his mane of blond hair as his body swayed rhythmically to his lavish bursts of laughter.

A magnet of bloody gorgeous male virility. Our confidant.

My superman hero. We clambered around him in the evenings as he completed his rounds, wishing us good night and briefing us on the next day's activities.

Lieutenant Herholdt accompanied us on the rounds of interviews and examinations, psychiatrists, nutritionists, doctors, physical trainers, each one a specialist in his field, examining, asking questions, filling out questionnaires, scribbling notes, adding papers to the ever-growing files. Always men, no woman allowed in the camp.

# Brainwash!

My first interview took place in a darkened room. Pulled down blinds blocked the blinding sunlight reflected from the salt pans. With my shirt removed and heart rate monitors fixed to my body I sat down in a recliner chair.

Lieutenant Herholdt told me to remain calm.

I watched as he took a syringe, filled with a dark brown liquid, from the metal kidney bowl on the table and pressed the needle gently into the dark vein running inside the joint of my left arm.

Minutes later I drifted off into a hazy world of real, unreal, surreal visions. I could not discriminate between what was in the room when I walked in five minutes ago, and the imaginary objects and animation my drugged mind brought to the table.

A soft, calming female voice from the ceiling speakers informed me a serious of questions were to follow. A yes nod or no shake of the head will suffice.

'Don't fight the impulses of your mind to hide or run away from the truth,' the female voice said. It was the first and last time I heard a female voice in Camp Basawa.

I nodded my understanding.

It felt comforting, reassuring, hearing a female voice, a voice not representing harshness, a voice not commanding, but telling, informing.

Lieutenant Herholdt pulled a chair up next to mine and laid his hand on my leg. Golden hairs covered his strong, suntanned wrists. A black scorpion engraved on the signet ring he wore on the little finger of his left hand.

Then the lights dimmed. I felt good, a bit titled.

A lonely sun ray thieved past the blind onto the floor.

The lonely wailing voice of an African female singer drifted into the room. I swayed my head to the music. Minutes ticked by.

Suddenly the questions started. I recall the first five or so questions, then the questions blended into a serious of nods and shakes of my head. The questioning continued a considerable time.

At times I hesitated, probing questions my mind, up to now, had spent little or no time considering. I bit my lip and tasted the acidic blood.

The uncomfortable questions asked about Abel remain vivid memories, they came in short bursts.

'Have you had sex with your brother?' I shook my head.

'Have you had sexual desires for your brother?' I hesitated, Lieutenant Herholdt squeezed my legs, I nodded, then smiled in his face.

'Kaner have you had sex with a man?' I nodded, feeling they reached for weak point inside me.

'Kaner have you ever killed someone?' I shook my head.

'Kaner would you kill a black man if you see him rape your mother?' I nodded. My heart beat faster. Was I giving the right answers. Now was not the time for betrayal of blood relations.

'Kaner, do you believe in God?' I shook my head. Then I ran in my mind. Oh Enola Gay rescue me to run so far away.

'Kaner, do you have fears?' I nodded. Then I ran in my mind. Oh Enola Gay rescue me to run so far away

'Kaner, are you of a pure mind.' I hesitated, Lieutenant Herholdt squeezed my leg, I shook my head. Was that a leer I saw on his face? I could not get away. Enola Gay stayed away.

Without forewarning the questions stopped. The wailing African voice stopped. An overhead projector started whirling.

What I felt was not relief exactly. An emptiness voided my mind, was this how people feel after spending time in the confessional booth?

Alas, it was not bloody over.

Black and white images flashed onto the wall. Tribal warriors danced around a fire. A white woman tied to a pole.

The whites of her eyes filled with fear. Painted warriors beat the drums clutched between their legs. Naked black maidens gyrated feverish around fires, their heavy breasts bouncing up and down.

Grey and wrinkly elders sang songs in high pitched voices. A sangoma stepped from a grass hut. Ostrich plumes lined his head gear.

Three black snakes wriggled around his neck. He raised the snakes above his head. The ferocity of the dancing increased as the drum beaters increased the pace.

The sangoma raised a knife as he moved towards the woman.

The woman screamed. Her screams incited the drummers and dancers.

Faster and faster.

The sangoma raised a dried calabash above his head and poured the liquid over the white girl.

He held the snakes in front of her face. With blinding speed the one snake lashed forward, sinking its large fangs into the cheek of the white woman. She screamed, the viper struck again.

The woman thrashed violently against the ropes. Her body slumped as the viper nestled around the neck of the sangoma. The feverish dancing continued. The movie reel stopped.

I gazed wide eyed at the white wall, the images continued reeling through my hind. The voice, there was a voice, a male voice interspersed between the music and images, was it the General's voice, I was not sure. The voice repeated the same word over and over, 'Karelia, Karelia, kill, kill, kill.'

I shook my head, I was not sure of anything, not of what I heard or saw or felt, I felt bewildered, but euphoric at the same time.

Lieutenant Herholdt took me by the hand and lead

me out of the room, his grip was rather tight. He sat me down in the shade of the five trees planted around the main tent and handed me a small cobalt blue bottle, instructing me to swallow the contents.

I would rather want strawberries and ice cold vanilla ice cream. Oh Enola Gay, let's run away, faraway from here.

A faint sigh bubbled up from somewhere inside me.

I felt an empty sadness like they took something from me I wished not to parted with. What they replaced it with, I was scared to investigate. In in all my life nothing more peculiar happened. Then I tilted like Joan of Arc in the hands of her angel queens.

'You will kill with your hands. You will feel nothing when you kill. Kill clean. Kill quick. Do not let your victim suffer. You are not a murderer. You kill to safeguard your nation. To safeguard the future and stability of this country for future generations. You will work in hostile environments. The government will not recognise your existence. Your name will not exist on flight records. You will be dropped under the cover of the night beyond enemy lines to find and kill the enemies of our land. The perpetrators of mindless land mine killings, infiltrating our country, seeking out to bring us to our knees. When you leave here you will be trained as one of the finest killers in the world. Never will you feel the need to glance over your shoulder, fear will not whisper in your ear, no man will lay a hand on your shoulder in surprise, other men will look over their shoulders as they walk past you, inhaling your killer instincts, their fear resting comfortably in your nostrils. Your senses will be sharpened, your prey will live with trepidation, more ruthless killers have never roamed this planet, you will join a global elite. You will not care about your opponents, only the killing, implementing your training, shooting a man on a street is for amateurs, you will exterminate targets on my command only, or if your life is under threat. Our enemy will feel we are upon them. We will crush their resistance.'

# Saturday night pretty babies!

I recall the tempo and tone of life in Camp Basawa
changed late Saturday afternoons and continued in the
same cadence into Sundays. Alternative syllabus classes
were taught on Saturday morning, six subjects on offer, it
was the only time of the week the classes were mixed and
we enjoyed the company of the other boys.

I choose Toxicology and Terminology, combining my
fear for snakes and death fascination into subjects
helping me overcome my childhood phobias after
lengthy discussions with Lieutenant Herholdt and the
camp psychiatrist.

'Trust your natural killer instincts,' I was advised, 'we
all have the ability to kill, it is the most natural and basic
instincts of human life, the desire to survive on this
planet as the ultimate goal of life is death, you give your
life to feed planet Earth children, Life. Do not fear what

you feel inside'

We learned from nature's most effective predators the art of setting a trap, luring them into a false sense of security in your liar before swiftly terminating their lives.

Abel choose Terminanology too, the specialist art to terminate life in the most fast and effective way. He also chose Tormentonology, the art of torture, extracting information from one's victim before killing them swiftly or leaving them to a slow and excruciating death, safe in the knowledge there was no return from the death abyss after the infliction of the most inhuman torture methods known to man.

For the most part foreigners delivered the Saturday specialist lectures.

Scientists carrying out deadly biological research in the international secret service agencies laboratories.

Foreign secret service organisation instructors demonstrated the black arts of information extraction, mental tortures and silent killing.

The preceptors arrived in black helicopters in the hour before sunrise and were taken direct to the General's accommodation, we saw them on the veranda enjoying an early morning coffee over intense conversation, barely aware of the boys scurrying about in black camouflaged clothes.

They mingled with us around the camp fires, engaging us in intense philosophical conversations, discussing life, death and the purpose of life with passion, quoting wise, ancient masters.

A new world opened, mesmerised and enthused I reluctantly went to bed after midnight, knowing by the time the sun poked its head above the parapet of a new day, the black helicopter would have transported its top secret passengers safely back to whichever exotic destination they had appeared from.

I, like so many of the other boys lived for Saturdays, for the privilege of being in the company of the finest minds serving clandestine Intelligence Directorates, Special Investigations, Military and Homeland Security, Control Bureaus. Men we viewed as romantic and mysterious, men leading a fantasy life, all with a single cause, protecting the security of the state and keeping the population safe in bed.

I burned with a desire for a first mission, my introduction into the exclusive world few men have the privilege to be invited too. How little did I know what fate awaited me, did Mama not always warn us, be careful what you wish for, but I wished, oh how I wished, little realising how soon my wishes would be fulfilled.

The Saturday morning lectures in the darker side of life, were washed away in the afternoons in the only luxury Camp Basawa offered its residents.

The swimming pool.

Homeless, moonlight sleeping on the midnight train. It was time to be boys again. Boy screams and laughter rang through the camp and travelled beyond the wire fence and across the dunes. Swim wear was not required and we were left to our own devices for the best part of the afternoon.

It was a time to socialise, make new friends, exchange tales and stand back in wonderment at the physical transformation life in Camp Basawa bestowed on our bodies.

The physical training and engineered food menus fine-tuned the body of every boy in the camp into a fine, lean and muscular specimen.

Abel developed a physique of a Roman god. I sat on the side of the pool one afternoon, minding my own world, my eyes fixated on my brother flat on his back on the opposite pool on his back, holding court amongst the boys.

Abel, the naturally gifted leader, had established himself as one of the most popular and trusted boys in the camp soon after our arrival, so unlike me.

I was not one for trusting too much, always vying with my internal distrust and the friendship on offer. My eyes roamed over his body. Water drops glistened on the black stubble and the long eyes lashes bordering his blue eyes.

His white teeth sparkled as he engaged in animated conversation with the group of boys crowded around him.

His torso smooth and chiselled from solid rock by a master mason, his stomach ripped, his penis dormant under a fine bush of soft black pubic hair. Then I noticed a tiny tattoo inside his groin, what could it be?

I sat upright.

This was new, I was sure, I knew every inch of my brother. The parts I did not know, I fabricated in my mind.

I had not swum the previous week, opting for an additional lecture with Moshe, a Mossad agent, in mixing venoms, but the tattoo was definitely not visible two weeks ago.

I watched my brother through veiled eyes. To my

surprise my penis became tumescent. I stared down at it in amazement, having given up hope of repeating the sexual excitement experienced with cousin Alex.

I pushed my swollen penis down as it raised its head like a sloth waking up from a peasant sleep.

Across the pool our eyes met. Abel lowered his eyes to my groin, he smiled, I blushed and sank into the cold, brackish swimming pool water, closing my eyes as I enjoyed my first natural, self induced sexual excitement since cousin Alex.

For the evening we dressed in shorts and T-shirts and gathered under the shade casted by the butterfly-shaped leaves of the Mopani trees.

Each boy was allowed two beers.

The fires burned high and the air filled with the fragrant smells of game meat cooked on the hot coals by the kitchen staff recruited from the local Himba tribes.

Soft music played through the speakers mounted in the trees. General Venter choose the music, a bizarre latin mixture, at first strange to the ear, but in an outlandish way it suited the unconventional setting of a camp fire in the middle of a passionless countryside.

The general adored the tango.

Dancing under the African sky followed supper. Dancing was an intimate affair, boys danced cheek to cheek, a slow waltz or tango across the dusty ground under a thousand stars looking down.

It felt natural, a spontaneous interaction as we left the week behind, the harshness and realism forgotten, we yielded ourselves to the secrecy of the night, for a moment time stood still and we were just adolescent boys capsuled in an inner circle of trust, something we rarely did during the week when we were taught to go it alone, not to trust, never to speculate.

On Saturday nights, for an hour or two, we felt another body close to us, felt a heartbeat, a warm breath in our necks, felt comfort, we draw on each other as much as we gave to one another. It did not matter, we were lead to believe we were special, shielded from the eyes of the world,

Abel and I were both natural dancers, the magical rhythm of music beats taught from an early age.

Abel and I danced with each other, and the other boys, leading and teaching them the steps.

The final dance of the evening was always a tango. Abel lead and I followed, we moved in a close embrace, our chests pressed intimately together.

Our heads snapped in time, I rested my right hand on Abel's lower hip, he steered me across the dusty dance floor, my eyes scanning the other boys and officers watching us intently, the fires reflecting brightly in their eyes, shadows swayed in the background.

The burning sensation in my lower body elevated me to a higher level of sensual awareness. The closeness of our pressed together chests subsided into our lower bodies as our hips thrust together, we followed the music with sharp pauses and rapid movements, our pulsating erections fleetingly in contact igniting a fire in my groin.The music stopped, a short burst of applause by boys and men standing and sitting under the trees.

I consciously moved away from Abel and sat down next to Marius, to a displeasured look on Abel's face.

I was not sure what happened between us, I needed time to decipher the physical emotions that had surfaced earlier in the afternoon around the pool.

Slices of watermelon were served to quench the dancing thirst.

The projector started whirling and motion picture images flashed onto the white sheets dangling from the branches, cultural education time, always Marlene Dietrich or Greta Garbo, the general's favourites.

He owned ten movies and we watched rerun after rerun. The dialogues were ingrained, the story lines recited by each boy.

I found it difficult concentrating on the screen and my eyes turned in the direction of Abel.

I studied his features, marvelling at the wonder of being his brother. Abel looked up, our eyes met across the flickering white projector light.

I jolted upright, I was in love with Abel.

An emotion as strong as the pull of the ocean washed through me, the world around me spun into oblivion. His eyes filled with question marks, sensing a change without understanding the nature, or did he?

My gaze returned to Shanghai Lilly.

'It took more than one man to change my name to Shanghai Lily.'

What now?

Sundays started with church service. The chaplain delivered his service, we sang psalms and hymns. The male voices soared across the salt plains of the Skeleton Coast. The service concluded and before long the heat sweltering heat descended on the camp.

I returned to my bed, avoiding Abel, not trusting myself in his presence, avoiding my platoon.

We were fortunate, our washing undertaken by the

Himba, we could focus on studying. My attempt at lettering writing futile, I was not even sure if our letters reached their destination. Nine months later and still no news from Mama.

Restless I jumped up and paced up and down the fence. The whistle blew for lunch. Cold meat and salads were laid out on trestle tables under the trees.

I picked at my food. Marius attempted conversation.

'Stop feeding Oubaas ostrich, the General frowns.'

'Let him.'

'You will go without food for 2 days if you do not heed.'

'I really do not care.'

'What's the matter Kaner, you look like the dogs took away your food.'

'I am giving it away, I always do, when I am not given away.'

Abel walked over. I stood up and walked over to Lieutenant Herholdt, leaving Abel with a quizzical look on his face.

'Permission requested to venture behind the fence Lieutenant.'

'You know it's not permitted.'

'I am choking in here, I need to clear my head, my thinking space is locked by the barbed wire. Please, I won't venture far, just sit on a dune, thinking, I need to get away from the others.'

He walked over to General Venter, turned his face to prevent me from lip reading.

Both men looked up in my direction, General Venter nodded.

'The General is permitting you one hour outside the

camp, I'll accompany you,' Lieutenant Herholdt said.

I threw him a dismayed look.

He hastily added, 'I will follow at a safe distance, go ahead, I will catch-up.'

I took the pass from his hand and strolled through the gates.

# My Aching Heart!

I headed towards the dunes, navigating my steps with care through the minefield, following the intricate pebble and thorn mosaic like a blind man reading braille.

The sun baked mercilessly, the sombrero protected my face, I was getting better at tolerating the sun rays. The camp doctor injected a solution increasing my resistance, toughening my skin. On the horizon a large white cloud shaped itself into a magical cauliflower.

No doubt nothing will come of it, the little bit of humidity the sun soaked from the earth, vanished long before rain could form. I had not seen rain for ten months. The heat seeped through my boots. I slowed my breath as I ascended the first dune. At the top I sat down, looking down at the camp with its rows of asbestos barracks, the tents, the little house of the general in the centre of Basawa.

Lieutenant Herholdt kept a safe distance, I called him over. He was barefoot. I was impressed. His initials engraved on the combat knife ivory handle resting in a rhino sheath on his hip.

I carried a boot knife, the only weapons permitted outside the camp, with the exception of our hands. From underneath my feet the giant sand whale forcefully expelled heatwave after heatwave into the air. I started breathing deeper.

I climbed the first dune and sat down.

I watched lieutenant Herholdt making his way in my direction. He took off his uniform and was dressed only in a pair of black shorts, like me. Officer's life did not soften him. He carried a black kit bag in his left hand.

'Lieutenant, I am glad you made it,' I said as he arrived. I was. Desert solitariness had a short shelf life.

'Call me Tertius, outside the camp.'

I stood up and we walked down the dune away from the camp. The sand seeped through our toes. Halfway up the second dune he stopped next to a green tangle of spiny plant. He bent down and broke the stem with great care avoiding the prickles.

'Euphorbia Virosa, poison tree' he said.

He cut a piece of the thick slimy stem and sliced it open. Inside two sets of veins ran.

'One of nature's perfect adaptations, drink from the dark green, but avoid running your tongue over the lighter green vein with the milky substance, it's pure poison, lethal to most human beings and used by the Himba as a hunting poison. Never bite into pudding plants, always carefully dissect and expose the water veins before drinking.'

On top of the dune we stopped, the highest dune within eye's reach.

Camp Basawa removed from sight, isolation wrapped around my shoulders like a comfortable cloak. The beauty of the land lay in its barrenness. No life visible as far as the eye reached.

We continued walking, not talking, but I drew comfort just from his human presence in this desolate space.

'What's in the bag?'

'I will show you in a while,' he said and turned to me, almost as if he had been waiting for me to talk first.

'Tell me what is wrong, something has changed in you, I sensed it since yesterday. Is it your brother, you hardly looked in his direction today? Sundays your face lights up when you are near him, your camp fire dance last night more intimate than usual, then you pushed him away, your mind drifted from the movie, several times, and your eyes.'

Does one dare confess loving your brother? I was not sure, but in Camp Basawa we were encouraged to talk about most things. Lieutenant Herholdt indicated we should sit down. I followed. He placed the black bag at a safe distance from us. Our knees touched - sensationally so.

'Your brother is an official black scorpion, did you know, we initiated him this week, he is ready for mission.'

'I noticed, what did he do, what does he have to do?'

'It happens, you pick the moment when it presents yourself, the general will never manipulate the first time, an amalgamation of your instincts and training. No chemicals, no injections, no instigated provocation.'

'Who did he kill?' The lieutenant shook his head.

'Listen to me Kaner, you are special, you have been chosen for very special reasons, more than the brute force and intellect of Abel. The school shrinks spotted your potential in the schoolyard, through observation, but time is of the essences, you need to reveal your true nature before the year is over, otherwise you will be send back, along with the others. I cannot rush you, but let your feelings go. Trust your instincts, answer the call of nature, that is why you are here. I know I make no sense but the moment is magical, frighteningly so. I sat where you sat six years ago, having this same conversation with my lieutenant. Stop looking so unhappy, go for it, unleash your potential, you have been trained and refined by the finest male minds in the world. You have the knowledge, take a leap into the unknown, the men around you will protect you, but they need you in the field, to kill, the reason the state cares for you.'

'Have you killed many......Tertius.' He smiled a forlorn smile and nodded.

'More than I care to remember or care to talk about. Never talk Kaner, never. The moment you, as a life form, terminate another life form is sacred, there is no justification in divulging the detail. The day you are up beyond the boundaries of the blue skies two souls can discuss the moment, not before. The living ones remaining behind will never understood. Don't ponder, we do it to make them safe, like wiping ant nests from one's home to prevent erosion of the foundations.'

I said nothing, fixing my eyes on the horizon as the sun readied itself for the end of the day. A lonely vulture swooped in the distance, did it spot a dying animal, a life running out?

'Kaner, the company of men is one of life's mysteries, especially men like you and I and the rest of the boys in your barracks. We are born to love our own, there is nothing wrong with it. You have to learn to accept it. Open your mind to nature's destiny, it is what make us special, what brought us here to this vast, empty land, away from the influence of society, their disapproving eyes, their judgemental tongues, here we do not need laws to protect us, we are a law on our own, you should be happy for the opportunity granted to find yourself and make peace with who you are. The road of discovery is a lonely one, one only you can walk, once you started, there is no turning back, otherwise you will live a false life.'

'But is it futile?'

'Life and love is never futile, not in the company of men, not between men, it transcends the human mind, it transforms the experience of life, here, drink this.'

From his pocket Tertius pulled two blue vials, the liquid the same brown brackish colour that were administered during my first interview. I drank without hesitation. I trusted the young officer, I remember the feeling of lightness induced the last time the liquid found its way through my veins.

Tertius spoke again, his voice a low tone.

'Men like us are different from the rest. You may have had the first realisations of being different, you just do not know what it is. Trust your instincts, for what you are now being trained for, instincts relayed through your senses are the only survival tools you have. Your hands will not kill, unless your senses are alert. Your senses will not be alert if you have inner turmoil. Never fear the company of men, for men despise fear, an emotion they cannot stop as they grow older. It is a coming of age emotion as they are no longer free to roam this planet and sow their seeds as nature intended. They become bound down by the hackles man devised for himself as they are tied to their mortal enemy, their long time partner who savages their needs.'

The liquid worked swiftly. Warmth unfurled in my abdomen.

'We are different, we find a partner to suit our different natures. Your choice will be derided, society judges by the law of man, Mother Nature does not judge, an inventor never judges his own creation. Like a lonesome male lion sweeping the Serengeti plains we hold our manes high, our roars leave them shuddering in their footsteps. We know where we are heading, for we are not tied to the destiny they created for themselves, we fulfil nature's intend. In the company of men true friends are rare to find, camaraderie easily mistaken for true brotherhood. Keep your true friends close to your heart but your enemies you take to bed, ravage them and if need be, kill them, for the line between lover and foe, in the world of men, is hard to distinguish, unless you are prepared to subject yourself to the will of another man. Ignore the man made rules of society and follow your instincts.'

Homeless the moon slept on the midnight train. The strong winds cannot blow from its tracks. The homeless boys gazed up at the stars realigning themselves. Did someone say something, was that a cry of an African mother alone in her bed missing her son.

# The Scorpion Tango!

Lieutenant Herholdt pulled the black bag closer and opened it with care.

He lifted two glass boxes out.

I watched transfixed. A cobra curled up in one, a black scorpion stood alert in the other.

The cobra head larger than a man's size twelve feet, the scorpion tail scraped against the glass dome, a tail treble the size of its own body length.

Basawa specials, engineered in the laboratories to kill with deadly precision, accuracy and swiftness, lethal poison producers, two deadly predators, cold blooded.

I watched transfixed.

'Watch, be alert, you do not want a kiss from these two.' He slid the slide panel lid off each box.

Both creatures raised their heads in the direction of the fresh air inflow.

Slowly the snaked sailed onto the sand. It stopped, hesitant, assessing the change in habitat. The cobra flicked a forked tongue, sensing the heat, distance, choice of prey. I sat motionless, mesmerised, grateful for the calmness the blue vial induced, without it, I would have been unable to face my childhood fear. The scorpion's tail erected, its claws raised.

The two beasts sensed each other, two gladiators thrown into a make-shift arena, no escape from this death fight, running away tail between the legs not an option for either creature, nature in all its glory, stand your ground and fight to live or die.

Cold lifeless eyes zeroed in on one another. Why, why, why. The scorpion swayed its tail, I couldn't help feel sorry for the little black creature, what chance did it stand, his David figure facing the cobra's Goliath. How did these little creatures, crawling across the infinite planes, view the world from so far below? Is that why they were such ruthless and effective killers, always at the mercy of their enemies, and now, what now, as they faced each other, would they walk away, choose to continue their desolate lives, rather than facing a death dual? The humans forgotten about, ignored, one threat at a time.

The cobra raised itself to its full height, the hood spread, sensing danger from the tiny, combative creature in front of it. The scorpion motionless, waiting for the first move. Suddenly it shuffled left, why? Enticing its enemy into motion? The cold black cobra beady eyes detected the movement, its mouth gaped open, tiny droplets dribbled from its fangs, with lightning speed it plunged towards the scorpion.

Swiftly the scorpion sidestepped, returning to its

original position, its tail curved, the stinger poised. Too late the cobra sensed the movement, the scorpion raised itself up on its front legs, its bullwhip tail swung across the chasm and lanced the soft folds of the cobra's loose neck skin.

A low dog-like growl hissing sound emitted from the gaping cobra mouth with the injection of the powerful poison stream.

The cobra stood suspended in disbelieve at the surprise stung.

Why, why, why. O laka lamma le.

The scorpion ripped its tail from the scales, with the blinding, invisible speed of a jet fighter it catapulted itself into the air and landed its stinger one more time behind the cobra eyes into the salivary poison storing glands.

It scurried away, stopped, looked back, assessing the fate of its enemy, waiting for a counter attack.

The cobra staggered back with a deflated hood. It turned its head in our direction, killer eyes filled with incredulity from the arrival of death on the doorstep, the deadly black scorpion poison racing through its cold blooded heart.

Did snakes have hearts?

The cobra slumped and limped-sailed across the sand, defeated.

'Twenty minutes,' Lieutenant Herholdt said, 'the cobra has twenty minutes left to live.'

Shudders ran down the body of the magnificent reptile, it jerked and rustled on the sand.

The black scorpion turned around and walked away. I jumped up and placed the glass cage over it.

We sat and watched the cobra convulsing in its death throes.

I sat there with the young lieutenant by my side, watching the sun set in the west and the desert silence swirl around us.

I made a promise to myself. Nhliziyo yami, nhliziyo yami.

Never will I underestimate my enemy and their ability in taking life away from me, even if small and pleading at my feet. I will show no mercy. I will crush their head so they do not rise and stab me in the back. Should they tower over me with power and devastation,

I will side step their deadly attack and thrust my poison with all my might into their bodies. From the battlefield of death only one victor can walk away. Like the gladiators of old, I will fight and love with equal measures, my hands I will train to kill and love men with equal passion.

I looked sideways at the Lieutenant's handsome profile.

Deep inside me a seed had sprung up, like a spring flower dormant in the soil, waiting for the seasons to turn, from where it will rise to realise its natural duty. I wondered what went through his mind.

'We should walk back to the camp,' he said.

'I am ready to kill,' was my reply.

I do not know why the words sprang to mind, spilling over my lips, a confident feeling stirred an unknown emotion within, perhaps from watching the death duel, perhaps the serum we drank, perhaps my competitive spirit or fear of separation from Abel.

'When the time is ready you will know and take

action.'

A beam of light appeared behind us. It cut through the eventide. Sergeant Snake on a dune opposite!

'Lieutenant, the General demands you return to the camp with the boy.'

We stood up and ran down the dune to the waiting sergeant dressed in combat trousers and boots.

'Let's race to the camp,' Lieutenant Herholdt said.

The sergeant took his boots off. He tied the laces and hung the boots around his neck.

We set off, racing each other up and down the loose sand, keeping clear of each other's tracks so as not to slow down.

The lieutenant outran us with ease.

The cool desert air soothed my mind, clearing the earlier cobwebs clobbering my mind.

I looked for the vulture, it was gone, feasting somewhere, picking bones. An idea formed in my head.

We missed dinner.

The general stood on the verandah of his house, the lieutenant went over to him, I headed for the dormitory.

The boys sat on their beds reading and chatting. The bedside lamps casted large phantasmic scorpion-like shadows on the wall.

They looked up as I entered, but I did not engage in conversation, avoiding the eyes of Marius following me to and from the bathroom.

I drifted into a restless sleep, my mind whirled with images.

Nhliziyo yami, nhliziyo yami.

Abel and a scorpion fought a death duel, the lieutenant sailed across the dunes leaving scorpion tattooed footprints in his wake, he kept looking up.

Croaking sounds drifted across the sky. The sounds all too familiar.

Nhliziyo yami, nhliziyo yami.

I looked up.

It was the Hadida.

The bird dived down, sinking its talons into the flesh of Abel, the face of the lieutenant turned around, Abel screamed with pain as the Hadida ripped into his shoulders, I screamed, opened my eyes and saw the shadow of the sergeant in the doorway.

Why, why, why. I stepped from the bed, lifted the glass cage from the bedside table and walked naked towards the door.

My penis grew rigid with each step I took in his direction. He smiled, turned around and walked outside, I followed him.

The camp was quiet.

I looked up the sky, the moon did not put in an appearance, calculating the hour of the night was impossible.

I followed the sergeant into his room.

I stood in the door watching him drop his shorts onto the floor.

His penis, like his body, was oversized, fleshy and rock hard. The roar of the lion sounded up somewhere in the dunes.

I walked over to the bed and placed the glass cage on the bedside table.

The sergeant stood watching me with silent anticipation.

I held his gaze as I stroked my body, enticing him into the first move. He stepped over, scooped me up into his arms, placed me gently on the bed and lowered his bulk onto me.

The lonely lion roared again, in synch with the grunts of the sergeant.

I surrendered to the desires of my flesh, slipping out of my boyhood skin, like a snake I rubbed against a hard object, causing my skin to split, I crawled from my old skin with a loud groan.

With a single, swift movement, I slipped from under the bulk and straddled the hulk of a man.

His eyes pressed closed, his mouth hung open, spit dribbled down the mouth corners, I felt nothing but repulsion as he reached his sexual heights running his callous hands over my firm, youthful body.

A look of ecstasy on his face.

I reached for the glass cage, opened it and dropped the back scorpion onto the ecstasy ravaged face.

Without hesitation the scorpion lashed out, sinking its cocked stinger with rapid succession into the eyes of the sergeant.

The sergeant opened his eyes in astonished bewilderment.

He did not know what happened, his mind trying to work out why the pleasurable experience was interrupted with punches of pain.

Horror washed over his face as he caught sight of the large claws. He tried writhing from underneath me. His mouth gaped open.

The poison river waded with devastating effect through the human landscape.

Blinded he tried wiping the scorpion from his face, the scorpion stung into the side of his hand, Sergeant Scorpion screamed, I clasped my left hand over his mouth and commenced throttling him with my right hand.

The scorpion scuttled away.

The sergeant dragged me onto the floor. His body spasmed violently.

I crushed his windpipe, the bones cracked underneath my fingers.

Straddled over his body, for hours, I watched his life slowly ebbing away.

I did not release my grip, even as the big strong bully turned into a whimpering man with the black scorpion fever ravaging his mind, his swollen face grotesquely distorted.

As he blew out his last breath I brought myself to orgasm, his limp penis slipping from me as I stood up.

The black scorpion sat in a corner, fearing the day light, its hunting hours over, looking for a burrow to crawl into and rest.

I crushed it with my bare foot and placed its remains on the chest of the sergeant.

Nhliziyo yami, nhliziyo yami.

I showered and stepped outside. The morning star kissed the night goodbye.

In the east the first rays of the sun lit up the horizon. Sea mist shrouded the dunes to the west.

The land around me looked untouched by man, its mysterious beauty barren from life. The only sign of life was the white smoke drifting up from the kitchen chimneys.

As I walked over to the dormitory a movement caught my eye.

The general stood naked in front of the bedroom window.

I did not acknowledge him.

I laid down on the bed, awaiting the sergeant's bulk to appear in the doorway, waking us up for the start of a new day. General Venter rose our barrack from the deep Sunday night sleep.

His commanded, not the roar of the sergeant. The boys jumped to attention at the sides of their beds, not daring rubbing the crusts from their eyes.

I stood in the shower, cold water running over me, how long I stood there, I had no idea, I was unable to wash the images from my head. Monday morning proceeded as if nothing happened.

## *Tattoo!*

**Speculation** about the sergeant's whereabouts were rife. By midday I was called from history lessons and escorted by Lieutenant Herholdt to the building where my first interview took place.

We entered the same room.

The blinds drawn. Two trolleys stood side by side. One trolley empty, on the other laid the naked body of the sergeant, the crushed scorpion rested on his chest. General Venter stood at the far end of the trolleys with the camp doctor next to him.

I stared at the face of the General, no sign of his thoughts or emotions could be detected. Lieutenant Herholdt moved me by the elbow in the direction of the empty trolley bed and commanded me to undress.

I did as I was told, folding my clothes up neatly and placed them on the floor.

I climbed onto the bed. The sergeant's face was a dark purple and completely dysmorphic.

Little sign was left of the man guarding us on the bus ride from Peaceful Glen to Camp Basawa. The ceiling lights glared down mercilessly.

'This will hurt,' the lieutenant said as he pushed my legs open.

The doctor stepped forward. From a small leather bag he raised a small tattoo machine in his gloved hands. A whirling noise filled the room. The lieutenant pushed my flaccid penis aside.

I did not wince at the first stab of pain as the doctor pressed the needle into the soft flesh between my thigh and groin. My eyes locked with the General's pale blue eyes for the duration of the sculpting.

My penis filled with blood again and laid rigid against my stomach. Lieutenant Herholdt gently pushed my penis away from the needle and down between my thigh and groin.

My eyes locked with the General's pale blue eyes for the duration of the sculpting. My penis filled with blood again and laid rigid against my stomach. Lieutenant Herholdt gently pushed my penis away from the needle.

I closed my eyes and gave over to the sensations and images filling my mind.

As the doctor said done, I ejaculated for the second time that morning.

I opened my eyes, the lieutenant wiped me dry and helped me back onto my feet. I looked down.

A tiny black scorpion was tattooed in my groin. Its tail erected, the tip poised above its head.

Why, why, why. The end of its tail grew two razor

sharp fangs. It was a delicate, a precise work of art.

I picked my clothes from the floor and started to dress. I saluted the general.

'Welcome to the Black Scorpions.'

Nhliziyo yami, nhliziyo yami.

All three men shook my hand.

'Do you have a special request to mark your joining of the elite rank of white men in this land,' the General asked.

'I want to grow my hair and beard.'

The General nodded his agreement.

He walked over to the cupboard in the corner and removed a purple leather cape. The cape he draped over my shoulders and pulled the hood over my face.

Was it moisture I detected in the old lion's eyes as he cupped my face between his hands, his voice whimpered when he spoke:

'Go forth my son, make me proud, you are a natural born killer and the sunflowers will bow their heads with respect each time you pass in front of the morning sun, for at the end of the day we are children of the wind, may your dreams come true, unlike mine. You are a flower, even if an evil one, my Fleur de Mal. Who would have guessed something so dark would sprung from an afternoon awash with sunshine and red wine? I have nothing more to teach you. I leave you in the hands of the harvester of souls.'

He kissed me on the forehead, the pushed me in the direction of the door.

'Kaner,' the General called as my hand came to rest on the door handle. I turned around.

'The killing of people is a diabolical business centring

around madness and murder. Wear you magic amor robustly each day, never take yourself too serious and you will make everyone proud of you.

I nodded. Behind the General the doctor pulled a white sheet over the body of the sergeant.

I flinched as the bright desert sun light hit my eyes.

'This was a dual General,' I said.

'Duel to death,' he replied.

'What will you do with his body, unmarked grave?'

'Nameless. Plenty hungry desert predators out there.'

'I heard the lions.'

'Take time out and introduce yourself,' he said looking at me with a smile, 'you'd surprise yourself how good the night feels around a camp fire with an old lion.' He winked. I wonder what on earth he meant.

'Can I go General?'

'You may young Kaner,' he said, 'I trust you. You are young, make the most of it.'

'Thank you General, I will do.'

I saluted and walked from the room. Outside I stepped onto the parch ground. The History calls boys spilled out.

Under the tree a the lunch queue formed.

I raised my shoulder, from somewhere inside a sigh escaped. I stepped outside on the parched ground. The history class was finished.

A lunch queue formed under the trees.

I raised my shoulders assisting the rising of a sigh from deep within to the surface.

Lieutenant Herholdt grabbed me by the arm just as I walked away. In his hand he held a file.

'This is for you, its' time for the heat of the moment,

forty eight hours from now.'

I looked at him stunned. He smiled and winked.

'Congratulations, welcome to the Killing Fields of Fabuloso. The General and I will accompany you and your brother.'

'Abel too!'

'Hmm, you too impressed.'

He slapped me on the bum, then pulled me close against his chest. I realised my heart was beating in an awful exciting way.

I felt so aware of his body, his other person's smell. For a moment I held my face up to him for a kiss.

Lieutenant Herholdt slightly trembled against my body, then mumbled something and walked away.

'We are going to be alright,' he shouted over his shoulder.

I opened the file. The photo of a boy my age stared at me. A rush of bitter bile rudely brushed up from my insides.

Instinctively I knew this one I'd face in a few weeks to kill. I started to read when at the very moment, a large yellow butterfly came fluttering into the tent.

I watched it. It flew not with a funny notion, but a smiling notion. This was not an oops, and whoops butterfly.

This was a butterfly, like the boy in the corner, filled with unanswered questions about life.

It came to sit on my arm, I touched it tender green veins. I understood too soon it was released from the cocoon.

With speed I lashed out. It wanted to flutter and escape, I permitted it not. Around me dark creatures closed in on me. Entranced I stared, never before have I felt so high. To the ground its little body smashed. I stepped outside the tent and looked at the moonless sky.

'Is death upon my head,' I whisperingly asked.

From the great plains of the desert, the voice of the wind burst forth, 'You shall be lucky to see the sun again.'

In that moment I folded my wings around my vulnerable soul and with a sigh, I died a silent winter death as the low golden voice of Mama Africa whispered into my ear, 'You are the master Kaner. Peruse your instincts. Let it rise to the surface. Don't force it. I will never abandon you.'

There She stood, a vision of loveliness. I fell to my knees.

My fourteen year old shoulders sobbingly shook. Misery spewed forth from somewhere deep inside of my. Long overdue tears powered down as I looked into the face of Mama Africa.

But she was gone!

Did she feel overpowered by me? Only an abyss remained. The abyss stared back at me. A voice whispered.

'Looser. Looser.'

I clasped my hands over my ears.

'You possess no friend, no lover, you are a nothing and should be stoned to death.'

'No,' my voice cried out.

There he suddenly stood. The little thing science struggled to explain.

'If reason is your game,' he said to me, 'you have no place in my life.'

'What shall I do,' I asked.

'I'll always be with you, but your brains needs chemical reason to understand the pre-programmed meanings of your life.'

'Do our chromosomes match,' I asked.

All the tiny thing said, floating off into the night desert sky like a peace lantern, was, 'Science struggle, you will not.'

Overpowered I fell asleep. The last thing coming to my attention was the syringe needle slipping from my arm into the desert sand, still warm with the day.

From the corner of my eye I noticed the little black scorpion moving forward. I wanted to, but I could not move away.

Overpowered with silent angst in my eyes, I watched the scorpion lifted its tail to injects its poison into me.

Nhliziyo yami, nhliziyo yami.

Why, why, why.

## Scorpion Warrior

I laid my eyes on Bokero seven days after the third scorpion was delivered. The warnings had not been heeded. He sat on the wet mosses, the rarest of species, only to be found in the deepest forests of east Africa.

I startled him when I stood up from behind the shrubs where I awaited his arrival. I was fascinated by this ragamuffin, the strips of the fabled cloak fluttering behind him as he walked through the forest.

Bokero was regular as clockwork. He never deviated from his ways in the two days we observed his every movement. I was nervous, I secretly drank half a vile of the brown liquid in readiness for the encounter with my first target.

'Bayete Bokero Fezela,' I greeted him. He recoiled, when last did he hear the sounds of the Zulu language?

'Rutuku, rutuku,' he mumbled as he pointed at my

arms.

'He thinks you are a white man, European,' General Venter whispered in my earpiece, 'move forward, he has never seen a white man before.'

I touched his arm. His skin was clammy. The butterfly cloak brittle.

'Do not be afraid Uvevane Boy. I am your friend, an angel coming to rescue you from his hellhole in Africa, I will set your spirit free, return you to your beloved Bayali.'

'Unkulunkulu' was all he said, his eyes roamed my face, his knobbly fingers with broken fingernails stroked my face. His breath stale.

For a moment a unloving kindness welled up in me. I suppressed it. This was the enemy. My mind raced through the notes in his file, each line engraved, for I read and reread the file night after night, absorbing each detail in preparation for my first assassination.

A photo of Bokero did not exist, only photos of the marred faces of his victims glared up from the pages in the file, faces no longer capable of the most joyous human emotion. They opened the letters addressed to them with great excitement until the light of day was extinguished from their lives with a blinding flash of light.

I took his hands in mine, the hands of a killer, a mass killer, I stroke the four fingers, suppressing the urge to pull my knife from its sheath and slice the fingers off. I needed to be sure this young man was the letter bomb fabricator.

The intelligence sources struggled piecing the story together. All they knew was somewhere in the dark recesses of Africa killer letters were dispatched with irregularity.

A killer with a dark mind. The scattered pieces of the letter contents revealed cryptic clues of the mind controlling the assembling fingers of the killer. I was intrigued. In my dreams a dark shadow loomed, a faceless killer licking envelopes sealed with the blood of his victims.

I knew I should despise this man standing in front of me, but I couldn't, he was slightly older than me, maimed by life, without family roots, as far from his ancestors buried in the soil of Africa as from where he was abducted across the warm waters of the Indian ocean into the jungles of Africa. The little scorpion turned butterfly unfurled its wings on the warm gulf air, transporting himself to start a cruel assassination campaign against my people.

I had little choice, at any rate choices were not mine to make for a long time as others decided over the destination of my life, they knew my fears and insecurities and until I overcame my fears and insecurities, their manipulation and control stopped me from finding peace within.

'I must go, I will be back, tonight, wait for me, siyobonana masinyane.' I was not sure he followed, or heard me as he continually muttered 'Unkulunkulu' which meant creator of all things, did he think god was white, the world created by a white man?

I let go off his hand and turned my back on him. I walked back into the dark forest, leaving the empty looking face staring at my back, not sure what transported just now in his life, his magical meeting with a creature of the purest race, he did not know that for the first time Bokero saw the face of one of his victims.

The image of the young man with the long black tresses and finely trimmed black beard flamed into his mind as conflicting emotions raged through Bokero's mind. A reminder of the country he could not return to, a country where the body of his beloved Bayali burned to ashes, her bones cleaned picked by vultures turned brittle under the harsh African sun.

The squad of four waited the time out high up in the trees, each one lost in thoughts only known to him. Abel, General Venter and Lieutenant Herholdt and I. Our different tasks specific and detailed.

The lieutenant had been on scouting duties for more than two months, blending in with the locals, Abel was responsible for the termination of Masupu and Xen Xiu, I would kill Bokero and General Venter was responsible for our safe escape from this oppressive place, way beyond enemy lines.

Day light filtered through the tree canopy. I was not at ease, fearing snakes appearing on each branch. I rocked backwards and forwards in the fading day light.

All hell would break loose the moment the four us were back on board the power dinghy for safe transportation to where the Simon Town submarine awaited our return in the warm and shark infested waters of the Indian Ocean.

On this resistance pit-sore a rain of missile fire would be released from the B52's droning through the night sky on route from an unknown destination.

Our international friends never wanted it to be known their public disgust of our racial policies was nothing more than lip service, the prime minister never wavered in his support, or was it mere retaliation on his part, for was it not the current monarch that sold out the richest outpost in exchange for the  most precious stones from the big hole in Kimberley? All things in life have a price, even the lives of subjects.

I kid you not - our glorious finger swinging prime minister personally guaranteed a safe house for all the Boss' secret agents tasked with retaliation of the black bastards responsible for the crumbling of the greatest empire of them all.

The decline was unstoppable, but at least one could pretend and meet out revenge. The Air Marshall plan offered air support in exchange for the murder of targets their own secret services agents could not be implicated in.

The four of us did not talk about what lay ahead. The blue print for the night endlessly rehearsed and discussed before we infiltrated the forest, as far as we knew along the same route the abducted boys were transported. At midnight we each drank a cobalt blue vile, tied the black scarfs around our heads and climbed down the trees, lightweight backpacks secured on our backs.

The full moon shone high above the treetop roof, illuminating the path we were following.

The midnight monkey chatter obliterated the sound of our foot fall on the soft moss.

Were they on alert and spreading warnings, from the safety of their outlook posts, of midnight human creatures traipsing through the jungle? The sporadic squawking of a lonely macaw, unable to sleep, disrupted the monkey chatter. In the distance a lonely tribal drum beat a faint rhythm, warning the villagers of soldiers on the move. Mothers moved in darkness to protect their young from abduction. Their arms already empty from raids launched by bloodthirsty fighters.

Guarding duties were not taken seriously at the training camp and it was with ease Abel and I cut the wires and slipped into the compound. Few lights burned in the buildings. In the guard house two young boys slumped over their AK47 rifles on a table covered with discarded newspapers and dirty plates. A yellow light shone through the window of the camp commandant.

All very sloppy, how did they get away with it all? Making all those bombs, the bastards should have been taken out ages ago. I suppose the waited for me. Kaner The Killer. KK, perhaps I should have it branded on a T-shirts and become a superhero.

Abel and I stood for a few moments, starring at each other, knowing this may be the last moment we saw each other, for the instructions were clear, if you get caught, you will not surrender but without hesitation, swallow the vial with the pale yellow serum, a quick death preferable to the alternative, barbaric torture by the black children of Africa, their tribal instincts making them masters of savage torture rituals.

There was no point in being hacked open and one's entrails removed with pangas. A slow torturous death was guaranteed once information was extracted.

The effect of the brown liquid wore off after 24 hours, leaving the fibres of the nervous system overexposed and vulnerable. Abel and I hugged and placed our right hands on each others hearts, the unspoken vow of brothers in battle, allegiance until death do us part, we transferred the calmness of our heartbeat to each other.

'Love you brother,' I said, squeezing a single tear from

my right eyes. 'I will see you in homo hell if I do not get alive out of here.'

A look of surprise spider crawled over the face of my brother. A scrupulousness washed over me, as if some divine creature commanded me to say what was on my mind in these the final dramatic moments of my life. I nodded with a sly smile.

'Well I might as admit I am a penis lover. I saw you and Matt in the showers, since then, I cannot stop having sexual fantasies.'

Abel opened his mouth to say something, then shut it again. Was it my imagination or did I detect a naughty glint in his eyes.

He touched my perky bottom, then scurried away towards the grass hut where the petite Xen Xiu tossed in his saki and opium driven dreams of Geisha girls running around in scantily clothed rice paper dresses.

I watched his broad shoulders vanish from my way. Then I turned away from Abel and crouch-ran along the barracks filled with sleeping boy soldiers and their guards, their dreams filled with longing for homelands scattered across the African continent.

## *Die! Die! Die!*

The cost of sanctions and black market trading left the white rulers with an increasing arms and international shopping bill. The ransom demands of the African leaders increased.

Cargo planes filled with gold bars and bags of diamonds flew across the deserts and jungles of Africa. Concealed killers, trained in the finest educational facilities funded by the white Broederbond, parachuting down long before the landing gear was released.

I stopped at a few windows.

Rows of little black boys, between the ages of five and eleven, tossed and turned restlessly in their sleep, pining for the lap of a mother to rest their weary heads in. The ones with open mouths displayed rows of white teeth. The full moon shone bright on their angelic faces.

I shudder and shook the feelings of niceness off. I swiftly move through the dark. Needles and pins punctuated my feet. Somewhere in the jungle an orangutang farted so loud, all the birds started squawking at the top of their voices.

I kid you not. I was so totally loopy-da-loop off my fay head. In the jungle at night anything is possible, absolutely ducking thing.

Bokero sat bowed over his desk. I stood outside in the dark, watching the goose feather quill scribbling in a lopsided manner reminiscent of a crab dancing to a full moon sonata.

Stealthily I walked around the rondavel and slowly opened and closed the door. I stood quietly, scanning the room. It extraordinarily smelled. Stifling smell of potatoes fried in crocodile fat.

The room was small. The sloping ceiling stained with damp patches. A colony of mosquitoes sat in the one corner.

A moth with a death wish circle around the slow burning tall candle stuck into an empty Coca-Cola can.

Volumes of papers were stacked up in the corners. Dead butterflies were scattered across the floor, dry bristle butterfly wings pasted on the walls.

The tattered and faded white speckled orange and black cloak hung from the hunched shoulders of the boy-man scribbling away by a lonely burning candle.

Bokero looked up into the window.

Our eyes met somewhere out in the dark night as our ghostly figure reflections encountered in the darkened glass.

His oversized and flat nostrils flared like a wildebeest preparing for an attack.

Slowly the bomb maker pushed the chair back. The legs screeched over the floor smeared with cow shit. My hand sank into the pouch on my web belt. My body started trembling.

I was ready for a big surprise from this retarded sneak in front of me.

My inner voice urged me to unleash astonishing violence on this decrypt figure.

Suddenly without forewarning I felt nothing more but coldblooded repulsion.

He turned around, the butterfly winged cloak strips billowed out around him.

He looked rather goofy. His bulging eyes idiotically fixed on me. His eyes full of not understanding. He grinned disarmingly, then winked. He did not seem at all surprise to see me.

'What the fuck,' I said, did he look upon me as a potential ally?

My fingers touched the syringe filled with lethal snake milk and killer honey brew.

Underneath the tatters the butterfly boy was stark naked. His shiny black body slim and firm.

His skin glistened in the flickering candle light. No doubt he smeared some kind of animal fat all over him to ensure his skin in later life does not crack.

Moshe told me there was this famous black woman who said black never cracks.

Moshe and I laughed our heads off, 'what a magnificent lot,' I said. I hope to have the pleasure meeting her one day and share a phial with her.

My eyes dropped to his erotic parts. I inclined my head slightly.

A multitude of black curls spiralling wayward above his eminent manhood, reputed in the Zulu tradition as the first criteria for selection to the royal household of the finest Zulu king ever to rule the green grass highlands of Natal.

A king with a taste for the fine impis of his legendary armies, he never spent too much time in the kraal with his wives, for why would a man stay at home when he could roam the wide expanses of the land with thousands of young, virile men.

I pulled the syringe from the pouch.

Somewhere in the camp a cock crowed. Bokero stood semi-erected, he penis slowly raised its head like a cobra reading itself for an attack. The cloak slipped off his shoulders.

His physique slender, willowy, trimmed.

His testicles hung like two bodyguards behind his huge penis. I could not but to admit to myself his penis was beautiful, and his testicles.

'Bayete Kikuyu Boy,' he greeted me in broken English, 'you come to play with me.'

I stood stunned, then shook my head.

'You kill my people,' I replied in Zulu.

He shook his head, 'No, I am the butterfly boy, I sent light for the fireflies.'

Fucking dumb ass.

'I have to kill you,' I said, 'set your ngoma free.'

Silence, a few minutes passed.

'Aish, no,' he said in a pleading voice, 'my ghost must

be peaceful, if you kill me, my ghost will be restless until you hand yourself over to the police or die by your own hand.'

'You will die by the hand of nature and not mine.'

A dumbfounded expression appeared in his eyes, he did not comprehend my words. His chest heaved faster and faster.

'All these papers, is this all your writing, what do you write about?'

'The stories in my head.'

'What are they about, your life here in this camp?'

'Dreams, babazeka dreams.' His dreams were beautiful.

'In my dreams I fly on the back of a Hadida, away into a weird, imaginary world, do you understand?'

I was not sure he understand, I didn't think imaginary and weird existed in the Zulu vocabulary. They explained life through mythological folklore, nothing weird existed in the life of the natives, perhaps the white man's world, the world of subjecting black people to work in our houses.

How funny, our 'dominees' made us believe we were the Israelites, when in fact, we were more like the Egyptians, suppress, subject.

'Karelia, now, kill.'

The general's voice jolted out of my reverie into executioner stupor. The fine hairs in my ear tickled.

'Haa-haa-haa-de-dah,' he raised his arm along his side, flapping, imitating, 'Unkulunkulu fly with haa-haa-haa-de-dah. I fly with Impundula.'

'Aaah,' I nodded, it made sense, of course he would, 'beautiful, the lightening bird.'

The 'Hammerkop', fable bird, the black and white bird with summoning powers, it calls the lightening and where the lightening strikes, it buries its egg.

The eggs and flesh were used by sangomas for medicinal purposes, providing the sangoma with control over the minds of the tribes, the law-abiding and lawless.

The bird transformed itself into a beautiful young man and seduced women.

He nodded, a strange connection between us, this black man with the soulful but emotionless eyes.

'Karelia, kill.'

The voice whispered, this time more urgently. 'Smash the serpent's head.'

My heart raced.

The sea rushed into my head, waves crushed over my mind, blood drained from my face.

Then my heartbeat slowed as the waves pulled back leaving wet, calm sand behind.

I stepped into the wet sand, my feet sunk away. The night air felt cool against my skin. I stepped forward and grabbed the Butterfly Boy by his genitals with my left hand.

My fingernails dug into the hard penis flesh. I yanked him towards me. My right hand plunged the sharp dagger of honour needle into the soft fat free stomach fold.

At last!

The white viscid mucus substance projected from the syringe into the black boys' entrails. With eyes wide open he stumbled forward.

His claws reached out for my scarf. He slumped against my body as his legs turned to jelly.

Die bastard die, like the little girl you maimed. It felt good.

I felt good. A broken smile broke over his moon face. His lips mumbled something.

I understood not. It felt Bokero handed himself over, perhaps he sought release, escape from this four-walled-prison where he was trapped so far from his motherland.

I lifted his featherweight body and laid him on the bed as the first painful, violent convulsions hit his body.

His eyes rolled back into his head. His shoulders slumped. His riddled with poison body bleeding on the inside. His flat nostrils flared, his muscles contracted, his toes curled tightly as his body fought against the agonising pain.

I pulled the tattered cloak strips off his fragile body. I reached down and picked a pile of the yellow stained papers from the floor. His head rested on my lap. I stroke his curly hair.

'Karelia?'

'Mission executed.'

'Vacate now.'

Urine dripped spilled slowly from his full erected penis, a penis caught in death throes.

His penis fully erected by now. White foam trickled down his mouth corners.

His fingers rubbed over his eyes reminding me of the praying mantises Abel and I watched as little boys sitting amongst the reeds of the Elephant's river, catching frogs to barbecue over a fire in the field.

For the first time I watched and experienced the effect of the black mamba scorpion laboratory engineered poison on a human, having seen laboratory rats died instantaneously.

My name written on the blue vials developed for my exclusive use, my signature poison raced through Bokero's veins.

His skin turned ash-grey as the snake poison soared. The poison burning his insides with the same fierceness the sun scorched the earth.

The poison pillaged the body, the ebony skin fading in front of my eye to a ghastly grey. One by one the stars in his eyes died down. In front of my eyes a young man succumb to becoming a corpse.

Suspended I sat there. What are the desires of a dead body, I wonder. To rise up and vanish from this world, to separate the soul from the flesh.

For the tongue to fall silent and the eyes finally to close?

For the human sweetness to evaporate and return below the soil from where sweet smelling moonflowers will rise with each full moon.

Somewhere in the distance a lonely missionary church bell tolled the singular lonely hour that follows midnight.

My thoughts drifted to my brother, I wondered, did Abel hold Xen Xiu and Masupu after gouging their eyes out and severing their windpipes.

I doubt he showed his targets tenderness, mercy was not an act my brother indulged in without due cause. Bokero approached the valley of death slowly, the convulsions intensified, his breathing slowed down. Minutes of his life remained as the poison did its job.

The hourglass sand ran low.

Will he meet the little girl who opened her father's

mail in eagerness to please him as she sat on his lap after he returned from work.

The police found her eyes behind the deep red velvet sofa, next to the nose and lips of her father. I watched Bokero, his departure from this life so different from the departure I witnessed Sergeant Snake experienced.

I raised the yellow stained paper and read to Bokero his own story. I eased his way out, taking his mind off his own death, a concession his victims were never granted.

'Once upon a time, in a land, far from where I now sit to tell the story of a life that never was, lived a boy born with the claws of scorpion and the wings of a butterfly.'

A wry smile brokered around Bokero's thin lips. For a moment they turned upwards, his face lit up, his eyes opened.

I looked into the dark pools, pools filled with the memories of a young boy roaming the forests with his grandmother.

A life filled with tale of butterflies and the dark horrors of abduction. Never could he have dreamed of his life ending so indignantly in a foreign land. With every breath he took I watched him break his bond with life.

This was an unpleasant job, but someone had to do it. The destruction of my people I could not stand for.

'Jok.....it doesn't matter....Jok......thethelela,' his bleak thick lips falteringly whispered. In one long breath his final air escaped from deep within.

His naturally mutilated fingers let go of my mask and his arms dropped.

The Butterfly boy, turned Scorpion Warrior, whispered before a final merest breath of air escaped from deep within, over his thin bleak lips.

The four claws dropped from my face where they spent the last minutes of his life stroking the black scarf obscuring my face.

He felt the contour of his maker, his god, the one taking him away from his unhappy life, child murder, snatched from innocent childhood, he snatched the innocent lives of others.

His brave soul departed to the other side. His beautiful corpse, like an old European city, remained behind, a dead place to live in.

I pushed his eyelids close and pulled the cloak over his face and rested his head on the pillow. The scorpion boy died like an animal, in his game of fire, fire killed him.

I scrambled a pile of papers from the desk and floor and pushed it into my backpack.

'Time Karelia, get out now,' the voice whispered in my ear piece, 'hell without a fury will soon break loose.'

The rest of the manuscripts I scattered over the bed, covering Bokero in his own fantasies, preparing him for his funeral pyre.

I took the candle from the table and held it against the sheet. The tiny flame flickered weakly. I almost pray for his soul to be still in the room. It could have extinguished the flame.

Then it let the flame touch the paper, the bedding. Flames engulfed the bed and body as I walked from of the room.

I waited a minute.

Nobody was outside.

I leaped through the camp, running away from the

visions filling my head.

It felt like I ran in my own nightmare. At the edge of the camp I turned around, smoke, black, curled up into the night sky. The stars above obliterated. I rubbed my eyes. A scorpion, phallic majestic, rose from the blazing fire.

Upward it stretched, conjuring forms. Toward me it rotated.

Blazing its two top eyes turned on me.

Hissingly it shrieked, 'Devil child, spawn dust, can't you see, you are me. You broke our bond. I decree your soul descend into hell fires. Alone you shall be left in this world.'

I felt its hatred.

Then the scorpion vomited deliriously, over and over green slush spilled forth.

The flames hissed, ferociously it licked the loathsome exoskeleton of the gigantic predator. Right there in front of my eye it erupted and fell down into the furnace.

I slowly ran my hands over my face, ripped the mask off and dashed away.

Abel waited by the hole in the fence. In the moon light his hard face glanced at me vacantly, then pulled me close to him.

He held me tight for a few seconds. His heart beat fast against mine. His lips gently touched my ear. His hands caressed my back, lingered for a moment, then he pushed me forward to give pace.

We sat off on a hasty pace, the soft humming of the bombers audible in the distance. The general and lieutenant hugged Abel and I, shook our hands.

'Well done my boys, we are unstoppable,' he said

grimacing, 'let's get the hell out of this viper's nest.'

I was not sure what I felt. For now a feeling of nothing would do. Lieutenant ruffled my hair and grabbed Abel by the shoulder. Smiling he said, 'What a wonderful trip this was. I am so proud of you two. Roll on the next mission. Let's get on to that submarine, time for some barrel turning fun.' I stood perplexed and intrigued. To my surprise Abel understood the reference, 'Lieutenant, my timbers are shivering.' Is he proud of me.

## *Yellow submarine!*

**At** the beach three power dinghies awaited our arrival.

We ran into the shallow dark waters. The water caught the light of the moon, exalting the beauty of the night.

Far out in the deep I just about make out the small compartment of the conning tower poking above the twinkling ocean water. It was painted bright yellow.

The submarine body submerged for a speedy get-away. The HMS Amy Winehouse laid simmering in the dark water like a sinister whale-like spear.

Just as I climbed down the conning tower another dinky arrived. I was so excited about the undersea voyage.

The perfect ending to my first killing expedition. The black painted faces of the Elite UK Special Forces dispatched to place explosives looked up smiling.

Their task placing explosives around the training camp, targets around the local villages, power lines and bridges completed.

We warned the mother fucking terrorists, they heeded our warning not. I had no doubt in my mind the shit will fly in droves and the earth scorched to the ground. To quote, 'their timbers will shiver.'

Each explosive engraved as 'Allahs' bomb.' I kid you not - fucking sick the humour our guerrillas had.

We learned from the best, our former colonial masters. Pull your upper lip tight and blast the enemy to hell and back. One of them shone a torchlight in my face.

'Boys, look what we have here, the infamous assassins boys. My God, you Sally's seem to young to be outside your mother's womb. My timbers shiver.'

Again - that expression, why am I not in on the joke, or is the joke on me? I stood dumbfounded, who would have guessed Abel and I had a reputation with these ruthless men.

Something stirred in groin.

The one with the torchlight reached up, grabbed my arm. His fingers sensually warm on my skin. He was a lanky fellow with big intense eyes.

His head covered in a thick mane of hair. We faced each other for a minute or two. Something transgressed, what, I was not sure.

Was I honestly biologically wired to have sex with most men I came across?

There was something predatory sexual about him - not a male lover to be scoffed at.

Suddenly I was reminded of Admiral Nelson's diaries.
Life on sea was all about rum, sodomy and the lash.

'I shall see you later down below, Sweet Chilly Face,'
he said with a smirk.

He was cute. 'Let's see,' I said. Bringing it on sister I
thought.

I pulled free as a whistle blew somewhere inside the
submarine. I looked back at him, 'by the way, the
admiration is mutual, you are cute, even with your black
painted face. Come and show me your rugged features
once your make-up is wiped off.'

Cheekily I blew him a kiss.

Above my head a shooting star whisked through the
starry night.

Quickly I crossed both my middle fingers over my
index fingers and made a wish. One day I'd go England
to become a professional killer.

As payment I accept rum, sodomy and the lash.
Whoopee! No traditional life for me.

Just then, something in the water caught my eye. A
face, black and bright, sadly smiled up at me with dark
eyes, deep below the water I saw a restless scorpion tale
flickering on the hunt for a prey.

A half-hearted scream welled up from my throat, I
swallowed it back. Just then a scattering of fluffy white
clouds passed across the night sky. The silver light faded.
I looked up.

I hated it so much when my dramatic side overwhelm
me without any kind of forewarning.

Even by my standards I was an utter shambolic mess.
I saw the moon stowing away its face from me.

In shame, or with blame?

Hate or with spite? A desire to drop my head in my shame rushed through my being. I buried my face in my hands.

A hand dragged me down the ladder that drops twenty feet into the hull of bustling activity. Men were on the go, in and out of doorways and around passage. Lieutenant Herholdt stood waiting.

'No need for that,' Lieutenant Herholdt said, 'face up.'

From his pouch he removed a syringe. With his head he signalled I must hold my hand out.

I did so.

The needle slipped masterfully into the bulging vein.

'This will help, so you can enjoy yourself in this little stowage space under the ocean.'

He ushered me along the corridor, just as the hunky sailor lowered himself.

The hunk winked at me and vanished in the opposite direction.

As usual nuances escaped not the eye of Lieutenant Herholdt. He must have seen from my face what I was thinking.

'Behave Kaner, they will rip you apart.'

I put on my most innocent face.

'Enlighten me, please do.'

'Forced fellatio, these men are worked up from the mission.'

I grinned.

'Of course, glad to hear. Let's not forget I just completed my first killing mission. 'Worked up' falls extremely short describing my lascivious state, with every breath I take my testicles nudge my cock to go hot trotting.'

'I will be watching you.'

'Feasting on my bubble tight ass. You missed out Lieutenant, tonight this child whore is spoilt for choice.' The Lieutenant gasped. I relished his obvious conservative discomfort.

'You are expected at the dining table of Commander Woody tonight. No shenanigans,' he said tittering, 'put a plug up your butt, no crossing of frontiers.'

He might as well have spoken to the wall.

'Yes Lieutenant,' I said and saluted, 'tell me, is it true there is a navy saying, 'a grunt can't talk with a cock in his mouth?''

'Kaner, your mouth is filthy.'

I laughed and shrugged my shoulders, 'Story of my life, but in all honestly, filth seeped into my mouth only since my arrival in Camp Basawa, Lieutenant.'

Someone shouted at us to get on with it and move out of the way. We hurried down the passage.

It surprised me how familiar Lieutenant Herholdt was with the lay-out.

The sailors stood tall to one side to let us pass. Lieutenant Herholdt opened the door into an extremely tight space.

'Yours and Abel for the night.'

I looked at the tiniest of spaces with a single bunk.

'A private suite, all for me,' I gasped delightfully and clapped my hands, 'how very considerate of them.'

'You and Abel.'

'You kidding me, Lieutenant, I expected sleeping with the sailors and the reccies.'

"Hmmm, I did not think his ladyship would be overwhelmed by this broom cupboard sleeping arrangements.'

'Broom cupboard is a spacious thing! Look at it. I'd be lucky storing a feather duster in here.'

He smiled. 'You have a way of looking at things. Anyway, Commandants' orders. You and your brother are minors.'

'Such poo! We can kill, but not sleep with the real men. This will encourage incest, you know that? I sleep here tonight in my oversexed state, there is only one way the night will end.'

'What you bottoming for Abel.'

'Lieutenant Herholdt! Wicked shame on you!'

'I just…'

'There certainly is no misunderstanding in the meaning of your words my good officer.'

'Give it a break Kaner. God!'

I of course had no such wicked intention. The injection kicked in. I put my arm confidentially around the shoulders of the fair haired Lieutenant.

'For was it not Chekov who said, 'it seems the fair sex is at the bottom of it.'

'Totally taken out of context Kaner,' the Lieutenant retorted, 'Chekov also said, 'the devil is highly educated.'

'With hoofs and a tail behind him,' I filled in, 'I shall indeed raise not only my hoofs, but also my tail for my beloved brother Abel tonight in this cramped space.

'Best you sleep on the bottom then.'

'I have every intend. That brother of mine has incredible weight, he might just crush into my dreams.'

He closed the door behind us.

In the close proximity a sudden warmth from the young officer's body overcame me.

For a moment I thought me might kiss. My skin tingled, damn injection.

'And have you?' He asked with a glint in his eyes.

'What?'

'Make out with your brother.'

'No, you asked me upon arrival at Camp Basawa.'

'You could have lied, you are one of the best fibber ever to have passed through Camp Basawa.'

'Really.'

'Natural born,' he said laughingly.

I waited for his laughter to run out. Then knocked him lightly on the head with my knuckles.

'Lying is the anecdote to high morals.'

'Tough stuff,' he said.

I took a deep breath. It was tough to breath in the cramped space. 'This place is stale with humid sweat, and someone smoke here.'

'You wince about everything thing like some gaudy fringe cushion.'

'Lieutenant, even by your standards that is the most ridiculous comparison.'

'Well, we are sinking fast.'

Goddammit. He was right. The diesel-electric engines of the Daphné class submarine hummed.

'Oh well, let me guess where you sleep.'

A pleased-with-myself smile broke over his face as if he was busy watching the sun rise.

'No need for guessing, I sleep with the crew. Hot bunking as a matter of fact so you two ladies can have your own quarters.' Then he reached out for a pile of blue clothing. 'Here, your poopie suit. Dinner party wear.'

In surprise I looked at the blue overalls with distaste.

'Simple, easy to wear and practical, nothing gets caught in it,' he said with a wink.

'I can't wear that. Fancy me doing one of my legendary cartwheels in THAT! It will ruin the performance.'

'Oh you so can, and you so will. This is an order. And good luck with finding the space to even handstand in this submarine.'

I wanted to say something, but decided against it.

Just then Abel pulled the door open, glanced at us. The Lieutenant left summarily with an, 'See you at dinner.'

Abel's face look like that of thunder-puss when our sleeping arrangements dawned on him.|

Somewhere in the depths of the submarine the engines hummed softly, edging the vessel along the west coast of Syria back to our beloved Island Kingdom.

I smiled and shrugged my shoulders.

'Just like back home. I'll whisper you a bedtime story tonight.'

'Hmm,' my brother grunted. There was no space for us to manoeuvre, so I climbed on the bunker bed.

'What's with you?'

'I need a drink to wash away the dying eyes from in front of my face.'

A little man poked his face into our quarter and said we are expected at the Commander's table. Needless to say dinner that evening at the Commander's table was not a fraction of what I imagined it would be. No chilled sparkling wine from the finest Cape of Good Hope estates. No perlemoen soufflé. No grilled prawns and oysters from the icy cold Atlantic waters. But that's just me, and as you know by now I set high imaginary standards. Eight of us ate in the Commander Woody's private mess inside his quarters. We sat on padded benches at a bright green picnic style table.

## *Deep Diving!*

Commander Woody was a tall gentleman with handsome features. One of those men drawing attention.

I felt please to be in his company. It felt good to socialise. After a few gulps of brandy, I laughed with the Colonel of the Special forces - a born warrior, enigmatic.

Fascinated I sat and listened to his mission stories of leading his commandos on 'pay back' massacre missions.

He caught my attention when he told me, 'As a young man I saved enough money and travelled to England. I joined the Royal Navy. I just wanted to fight, travel and see the world.'

Listening to his stories sent my wanderlust desires rampant. I just wanted to grow up and get away.

This was fairytale stuff. Isaac Potter dreams come true. The Commander married an English girl and moved back to South Africa.

My eyes glazed over.

This man was pure genius. My mind was made up. One day I'll marry an Englishman too. I scoffed down the breaded chicken, taco bowls and oatmeal cookie.

Admittedly I drank a great deal more than I ought.

By the time General Venter toasted our mission, I was rather drunk. The General stood, and so did we with raised glasses.

Too late I caught myself standing with a rum bottle in the hand. I glanced around the table, but no one reprimanded me.

I was the youngest dinner guest.

'You gentleman killed in style tonight. You killed the vermin, their rotten souls now burning in the furnaces of hell, their evil blood staining this land, their freedom curtailed,' his voice cold as he spoke, 'our woman and children sleep safer tonight. With every breath they take their waking up in the morning is guaranteed. Our leader will be informed. He will honour you in good time. The message we sent today is clear, there will be severe reprisals. We will unleash a purge of our enemies. We will hunt them down and squash them like flees hiding up a dogs' tail. We will swarm like killer bees. And those countries harbouring terrorist groups to flourish, we will crush too. Kaner and Abel, thank you from the bottom of my human heart. I thank you. You remind me all the time of my young man days. After seeing you two in action tonight I now know the killing fields enter another golden era. Our nation, alongside world peace, is being tested, but tonight I am more optimistic than ever before we will win the war and set new assassination records. May the new chapter long continue, our oppression of dissent voices victorious and our rise be unstoppable.'

I felt lightheaded in the company of important men. Finally I felt I belonged somewhere. Peace settled in my heart, or perhaps it was the injection.

Fuck knows, I took so much. And I ate not for days.

Now my stomach was stuffed.

So long.

I looked forward to the night ahead. Abel and I sat listening to the stories told by the seasoned killers. Each one fearless in his heart, prepared to sacrifice his life for his country.

As soon as the stories started to repeat themselves Abel stood up.

'Generals, please excuse my brother and I. We thank you gracefully for the generous hospitality. We need some time alone,' he said.

I wanted to object, I was having such a good time, why leave now?

Then as one the men around the table stood up and saluted us. I accepted the honour, there is a time to bow from the stage.

The Commandeer handed us a bottle of twenty year old cognac.

Abel pulled my chair out, we returned the salute and walked out into the corridor to the singing of 'they are jolly good fellows.'

With our heads filled with the food and booze and adventure stories Abel and I retired to our cabin. In the confined cabin, which was rather narrow,  Abel and I stood, looking at each other. We could not move.

Onto the bunk we clambered. We passed the cognac bottle between us.

I suddenly felt silly and did not know what to say.

'I feel empty inside,' Abel suddenly said.

'Yes, I noted you touched not the pork pies and scotch eggs.'

'Did you see physiques of the Specialist Force blokes.'

'Yes, they are fit. I wish I could be more like them. Like really masculine.'

'I need to loose my tube, I put on so much weight. I reckon it's the drugs they give us,' he said padding his waist.

'You reckon?'

'Hmm, it kills my appetite. I was rather twitted tonight. I surprised myself being able to finish the job,' he said with a malicious grin.

'No I am different. My fat body that is, I reckon. Ain't nothing better in the world to give me an appetite.'

'Oh dear brother well you'd be a damn fool to keep taking it.'

'I did not tonight,' Abel said.

'What! You did your killing without the drug. What happened.' I turned my head in his direction. Nasty surprise for me. Abel stank of old body odour. Jesus Christ, what a dirty deck and I have to spend the night next to it. I might as well go crawling into the trash can and wrap myself in fish scales.

'Well the fucking dirty Arab surprised me. I peeped through the window. All I could see was an oil lamp giving off black smoke. There was no one under the bed.'

'Inside the wardrobe?'

'Simple furnishes, soulless.'

'Sounds awful,' I said trying to breath shallow breaths.

'It was.'

Abel promptly scratched his testicles.

He smelled his fingers. Holy apostles, when did my little bro learn these awful railroad manners. He saw I saw. He smiled sweetly. What a goof!

Somewhere in the background the submarine engines rippled softly.

'So what did you do?'

'Well, I thought I'll check inside the room,' he said with a frown.

'Yeah, then?'

'Sweet-potato, crispy curl curses. The mother-fucking angel waited behind the door for me.'

'What!' I was genuinely taken aback.

Abel shook his head, I passed him the cognac.

'Kaner, I am telling you now, I nearly pooped myself. The dirty Arab was the ugliest motherfucker I saw in a long time.'

'What did he wear?'

'What the fuck you ask me that for? I am talking life and death situation here.'

He poked my sides with index finger. I let out a little foggy yelp.

'Whatever, you did not die,' I retorted, 'I like clothes, you know I am a bit of a fashion fan. One day I will go to Cape Town and become a famous designer. My motherfucker wore a fucking dry-brittle cloak made from butterfly wings.'

'Jesus Christ, these fucking jungle rats have no dress sense. Mine wore shiny boots, pieces of leather wrapped around his big fat hanging titties like some stupid eunuch in Osama's harem.'

Abel uttered a short laugh, then broke into a huge

yawn.

'You think Osama bin Laden had a harem,' I said rather ingeniously.

'Oh yeah, he was a bit of little Arab street boy penis fiddler.'

'Says who?'

'One of the mad red-faced killers at the dinner table tonight.'

'Holy shit! No wonder the Yankees took him out.' I impressed myself with my intellectual insight in international assassination politics, perhaps one day I can become a General for the American Army if I fail in marrying an English man.

'Precisely.'

Abel and I stopped talking for a moment to think about what we discussed. I smiled.

'So did you kill the fuck,' I broke our silence.

'Yeah, the idiot strutted in pushing a knife in my back. I felt it piercing my skin.'

'What did you do?' I wanted to know.

'An angry silence grew in me.' Oh holy shit! I wished I was there to see my brother like really getting angry.

'Why?' I asked.

'Cause he surprised me, I hate being caught off guard.'

'So what did you do?'

'Well, there was a little bedside table, with the drawer open. Inside the drawer laid a revolver. I dived for it.' The tone in Abeles' voice changed, he spoke much colder now.

'Holy shit.' I tried not to laugh.

'Fucking empty!' He said gravely after a pause.

'What!' I sat upright and bashed my head against the

metal ceiling. Stars, stripes and fucking red blood triangles exploded in my head. My head felt on fire.

'The motherfucker came after me with his knife. His eyes bloodshot and all. He screamed like a mad man! You fucking Western trash. You Jesus fornicator. I stood dumbfounded,' Abel said breathing fast and furious.

'He spoke English.'

'Yeah, poshest English ever.'

'What did you do?'

'Well, since I know the motherfucker and I spoke the same language I raised my hand and said, 'Stop in the name of fucking world peace you mother-fucking cock-sucker.'

'Fucking hell brother, are you a low-hanging cocky crow or what!'

I was like so impressed with my beloved Abel brother.

'Mate, he stopped dead in his tracks! He held his knife free hand out to me.

'I am from Birmingham,' the idiot I must kill said, I kid you not!'

'Motherfucker Mary.' I could not believe what I heard. A fellow countryman!

'So we shook hands. I told him I am from Halifax. We chatted for a while, he told me he came over to fight with Isis for his gap year. Nice guy and all. Tall, muscular.'

Should I be jealous? I said a little prayer to Madonna, please don't Abel tell me he and the Arab masturbated.

'So what then? You two kissed, had a cuppa tea and then made love.'

'Haha, funny Chopper, really sick, but funny. No, of course not. Jesus bloody Simon Stanowski Christ, stop with the jealousy. It will eat you up like a cancer,' Abel said rather annoyed with me.

'Sorry, but then what?'

The suspense started killing me.

'Well I could have just grabbed the ghastly idiot by the crotch and thrown him clear to the ceiling and smash his fucking traitor head.'

'No fun in that.'

'Precisely, my sentiments too. I told him not to make too much noise. Said their camp was booby-trapped with audio bombs. If he screamed or yelled the bombs'd go off,' Abel said.

'Jesus fucking Mary cook testicles in a curry sauce.'

'Precisely. The Birmingham idiot sat down on the bed.

'Truce,' he said putting his knife down.'

'Jesus, you trusted him,' I said.

'Fucking now way man. I noticed the nervous twitch in his neck. The motherfucker dirty asshole was up to something. I caught on. On the floor laid an ammunition belt. We both dived for it. I kicked him in the face, his jaw crushed so loud, I feared an audio bomb may go off.'

'Jesus-Christ, you got some balls.' My hero worship for my brother intensified.

'Yeah, damn right, tell me about it. His right fist shoot out to thump my nose. 'Oh Marilou, you should not have tried that,' I yelled, 'I am going to hot-rock your stinking dirty lice infested maggot diseased anus. Now one touches Abel's face and get away with his life.'

'Jesus Abel, brother I respect you.'

'Yeah, damn right, this was war. So I stepped on the arsehole's neck, loaded the revolver, ordered him to lift the dirty rag leather skirt up, then I stuffed the revolver up his hairy anus and emptied every bloody bullet. It ripped his insides apart. He blew up in the stomach, face as if a blow torch exploded within him.'

'Fucking hell Abel. You are like so my hero. Quentin Tarantino could not have directed better killing instructions.' I fell back on the bunk exhausted from just listening to the story, 'that was kick-ass,' I finally said.

'Hmm,' said Abel, 'like an oyster I split his inside, like a bloody oyster.'

'Jesus Christ, and that without drugs.'

'Hmm,' said Abel. We laid still in a sweet silence. Our legs rubbing against each other.

'Hey Chopper,' Abel said after a while, 'how was your mission.'

'Not nearly as exciting,' I said.

'Hmm, I suspected that much, night big brother.' Before I could even think of returning his goodnight wishes my stinky-poo-sweaty brother's light snoring reached my ears. I took of my clothes, drank the last drops of cognac from the bottle. Suddenly my eyes felt heavy. I fell asleep with the smell of Abel in my nostrils.

# Chasing the sun!

'My beloved sons, the last years sped by with haste, the house emptier than ever before. Your sister, Mara, still too young and, may I add, too innocent to fill the vast emptiness left by the two young men I still have to introduce into her life. She is pretty, she embodies the finest attributes of your father, her mother and two brothers. Are you feeling the competition yet, my beloved sons? I think the godmother of beauty may soon have a different view on who is the fairest of them all. My boys, I miss you two, your antics with the handheld mirror. Kaner they tell me there are no mirrors in your new world, I do not even have the name of your camp, I will post this letter to an anonymous post box. But the relief washed over me when your letter arrived, informing me, I can at long last take pen to paper and write with news to my flesh and blood. I trust they allow you my news and do not censor the words of a mother to her sons. I called on the General for a light hand by his black-pencil brigade. I learnt of your decision not to return home for Xmas with a saddening of my heart, for time dragged on interminably last year - is it really three years since you left? Dina, I, little Amara and Mara are getting on with our lives. Many nights, I found myself standing at the window of your bedroom, not gazing at the lonely moon and dark sky, but at the empty beds, and I wonder where you two are, safe in bed or somewhere in darkest Africa hunting down the threats to our society. I never cry, I bend over and rip the sheets and blankets from your bed, leaving pretence of your sleep presence behind for Dina in the morning. Then I walk back to the cot next to my bed and I say my thanks to the nocturnal ears for filling the vacuums in my life. I trust my boys are fine and in good spirit. The photo you sent standing on the moonlit beach is displayed on my bedside table. Where were you boys? Your faces are barely identifiable behind the black scarves, Kaner, Abel, your eyes my sons, delirious and distraught all the same, your eyes haunt me from the night-sky every night. Kaner, you filled out, are they feeding you better food than your dear Mama? I love you my boys and am proud of the way you serve your country and our nation.

Well, I wish my knights in the black masquerading outfits a peaceful Christmas. You dear mother misses you both, more than you will ever know and pray for your safe return to Peaceful Glen in the near future.

Mother A.'

I folded the letter and placed it back in the rucksack, alongside the photo Mother Abishag sent of our little black haired sister, she was a Du Preez with her smiley blue eyes. I promised myself I would not read the letter again. It was Christmas Eve, I was entitled to miss my mother, twenty four months had run out since our departure in a blacked-out bus.

I looked at Abel. He was busy with the fire, placing branches in a waffle formation with a small fire-lighter underneath. I reached for the water bottle.

On the horizon Kuyu stood balanced on a single leg. He stared into the west where the sun lowered as the earth face spun away from it. He said he needed to plan the route for the next day. I doubt he was telling the truth. The moving dunes made planning a total nightmare. We worked with the coordinates the General supplied.

'Six days boys to get to your destination. A helicopter will await your arrival and transport you back to the camp, it will only wait one hour. Miss the rendezvous spot and slot and you fail. You will have to make your way back to the camp on your own without food, you are on your own if you fail this task, you and the desert creatures. If you do not show up at the camp, I will not come looking for you, nor will the army, you will be missing in action, understood?'

We both nodded, what else were we suppose to do? Whimper and request a search party after one week?

No way. Abel and I did not hesitate.

We accepted the challenge. The prospect of racing through the desert over the festive season was preferable than to visiting Mother Abishag, it suited Mother too, for if we were with her, a visit to Rest-and-Peace was unavoidable. We were her get out clause for visiting the in-laws, Abel and I were convinced. No discussion was required between Abel and I.

We were given twenty four hours to make a decision on a leader for our expedition. The BOSS gave us two choices, Lieutenant Herholdt or Kuyu, the young Damara camp kitchen help, always found in the kitchen, bent over the sink, scrubbing pots and pans.

A tough decision.

Abel and I deliberated deep into the midnight hours. Kuyu was without a doubt the better tracker and as a native possessed first-hand knowledge of desert terrain. Lieutenant Herholdt, on the other hand, was an experienced soldier and navigator and whilst the Camp Basawa high command may well decide to let us disappear off the radar, they would surely not dream of letting the same fate befall on one of their star officers.

We decided on Kuyu, just in case we decided to get up to something not in line with army command, Kuyu was a safe and silent bet not to blab.

The other boys boarded the blacked out window buses heading home, two years training behind their backs, many would not return, they decided on alternative destinies. They were jubilant, excited at the prospect of seeing their families for the first time in twenty four months, but they were boys no longer.

Abel and I received our ration packs. Enough food and water supplies for five days.

The only weapon allowed was a hunting knife for cutting desert plants and shrubs, decapitate snakes and worst case scenarios. The preparation days were bliss, we spent time together.

'Would you watch me die, just sit there and watch me die, stroking my hair, telling me a story?'

I asked Abel, the night before our departure as we sat alone around the camp fire, a couple of steaks sizzled over the coals.

The General donated a bottle of red wine before he took off in a helicopter for a meeting in Voortrekkerhoogte.

Lieutenant Herholdt departed shortly after the colonel in a fighter helicopter for a mission in Angola, or as he called it, 'to leave a festive gift under the tree of the MPLA leader's Xmas tree.'

Four guards and a sergeant were the last remaining occupants of the camp, the majority of the locals disappeared into the emptiness of the land for a tribal festive season at their settlements, I was not sure they celebrated the birthday of a white child. The scientists, well, they moved in mysterious ways, helicopters landed and took off at all hours of the nights.

'Maybe,' Abel replied, 'it depends.'

'On what?' I asked, slightly disconcerted by his uncertainty. I had no doubt in my mind.

'Your suffering,' he replied, 'if you squeal, I will slit your throat, but knowing you, you will most probably suffer in silence, staring at me with your big blue eyes before one last attempt at telling a story of an Apollo god who died in a noble way as he was carried away on the back of unicorn in the arms of his goddess mother wearing a moon halo around her snake tresses, leaving me alone, as you blow your last breath out, to decipher the underlying message of your story.'

I clobbered him against the head for making fun of

me.

'I would not and besides, there are no underlying messages in my stories, you always expect too many underlying meanings,' I could see Abel was losing interest in the conversation. I lowered my voice.

'I will kill you,' I said, 'I would rather see you dead than suffering.'

'How?' Abel asked, gazed into the glowing embers of the fire, his eyes did not contact mine, he only directed his voice at me. 'Would you do it with care?'

'Yes,' I whispered, 'you will never suffer at my hands my brother. If the termination of your life lands on my plate, I will execute my duty swiftly and with mercy.'

'Would they ever?'

'Who knows,' I replied, kicking at desert beetle crawling audacious enough crawling over my feet, 'I suspect they may do, if one of us no longer serve our purpose, or cross over to the enemy lines. I do not think the Boss will look kindly onto traitors. I do not think we can trust the General fully. We are disposable, like they expect us to dispose of our enemies, their enemies, enemies of the State. In my dreams the four fingered boy haunts me with his sad butterfly eyes. Do you dream of the men you killed?'

Abel shook his head. 'Who can we trust?'

'No one, Mother Abishag, each other?' I took his hand in mine and kissed each finger. I placed my palm and fingers against his, his fingers outstretched against mine.

'Instincts only,' Abel replied, 'Let us only trust our instincts, like animals, our sixth senses. My suspicion Mother Abishag wanted to rid herself of us is still not unfounded.'

'Abel, what are you saying? No!'

'A hunch, who knows why she did what she did, animals do it all time, rid themselves of their young, nudge them out of the nest, it is the most natural thing to do, it's just us humans who cling to each other, I don't hold it against her, we are stronger for her decision.'

Abel and I ate the meat with our fingers and washed it down with red wine.

The rest of the evening we exchanged childhood stories. We enjoyed the silence of the camp, the guards kept to themselves and Abel and I day dreamed of owning our own camp from where we launched daring attacks on imaginary enemies.

Christmas morning Abel and I set off. The rising son expelled the night shadows with the light of a new day, the sand dunes coloured orange, the sky azure blue, new promises filled the day as the mercury rapidly rose its heat curtain from the sand.

Abel and I dressed in black camouflaged pants and T-shirts. Abel pulled a hat over his head for protection against the sun, I relied on my beard and long hair. My skin was long accustomed to the sun, my baby milk sensitive skin turned desert black.

Kuyu dressed traditionally, a goatskin loin cloth covering his manhood, a quiver filled with arrows hung across his back. His skin was protected by a mix of ochre mud and animal. We did not tell him the deal we had struck with the General.

As far as he was concerned, we were back in six days. Kuyu declined the offer of rations, he planned on feasting off the land with the help of bow and arrow. Kuyu was on a sabbatical from white man's camp life, not a survival course. He was in his element, white teeth glistening brightly against his mud covered skin.

We trekked across the endless landscape with the little brown boy leading the way. His firm brown buttocks beating time.

Abel and I followed across the first set of dunes, avoiding the indents of Kuyu's footsteps in the loose sand.

Abel fell in next to me, we picked up the rhythmic pace of the desert creature. At times Kuyu outran us, speeding ahead to set his direction.

With hand signals, drawings in the sand and an array of click sounds Kuyu taught us the movement of the dunes. Abel and I stood in amazement at the thousand skeletons scattered along the coastline, Kuyu occasionally changed course and dropped down to the coast when he noticed we struggled with the inland heat.

How long have they been dead, how did they come to their end, whalebones, shipwrecks, elephant bones, oryx skeletons, death and ancient life co-existed in an eerie manner.

History preserved in a natural museum which few visitors departed from alive. The first night camp was set up at the bottom of a dune.

The desert was unpredictable, nature mysterious in her movements. By day direction was taken from the sun, by the night starry Milky Way constellations pointed the way.

Each day presented a new landscape, the sand moved around by the unseen gods and a thousand rakes.

At times the sand roared as we rolled down it, vibrating, thrumming in our ears, the desert had a life, it spoke to us.

Kuyu told us around the fire it was the spirits of the dead fleeing from their skeletons before the wind gods swept the skin from the bones.

A bright moon passed over us through space like a giant celestial warden. The three of us laid close together, watching in silence.

Kuyu clicked in his native tongue as he pointed at the heavenly bodies, his white man's vocabulary insufficient so we assumed he was retelling stories, like Mother Abishag told us as boys flat on our backs in Peaceful Glen.

In the immense desert heat, bodily functions suspended itself. Breakfast consisted of a few energy bars.

At the end of each day Abel and I heated the military engineered food on burners. Kuyu disappeared on a hunt for desert creatures which he skinned by hand after slicing them open with the arrow head.

He cooked the meat on firewood collected on the hunt. His dinners ranged from oversized beetles to desert snakes, each meal had a distinctive smell.

Abel and I were not convinced all the meats were for human consumption, but we understood survival was possible.

Day after day we trekked, alternating between trotting in the  morning when the air was cooler, walking at a slower pace in the afternoon heat of the day, preserving our energy for the final hours of daylight as Kuyu accelerated the pace before marking a spot where we spent the night.

Always the sun. Gleaming above our heads, burning

down, searing the land, sucking life, giving life.

Our water supplies were treasured possessions. Abel and I drank sparingly. Saving our allowances for night times, when the cool weather made instantaneous evaporation unlikely, our bodies acted as sponges, Kuyu drank no water. He chewed on animal pelts for moisture.

On the third night I was woken by a slow movement against my hip. A nocturnal visitor.

I laid still.

I sensed danger, the instinct of a hunter being hunted.

My fingers rested lightly on the steel of the hunting knife at the side of my leg. Death by sudden movement a certainty. My body heat, undoubtedly, a warm destiny for a desert snake on the prowl.

At the first sign of being made unwelcome, it would lash out, with speed and accuracy, biting the hand refusing it a warm resting place.

The broad, flat snout slithered over my hand, the cold smooth dorsal scales followed the head as its forked tongue flickered over my penis.

One wrong movement would cause my death, the injection of a single  median lethal dose subcutaneously by this cylindrical predator would donate my skeleton to the already oversubscribed Skeleton Coast museum.

I waited, my breathing deepened and slowed down, comforting the predator, aligning our heartbeats, my chest and abdomen barely rising, slow exhales.

The picture of Jaubert flowed into my mind, the blonde French Naval Commando agent, our autogenic training instructor, visualisations of departing from ones body, the conscious becomes unconscious, not even a rat will sniff at you, he told us, solar plexus disconnected, blocked, the nervous system suspended. Jaubert broke the five fingers on my left hand, shouting, 'you feel pain, mon dieu, this is not pain, relax, stop breathing, slow down.'

Each time I winced he stepped on my fingers, again and again, until I slowed my heart rate right down, the pain drifting away into a cloudless sky.

That night he took me to new physical heights where pleasure and pain co-existed, the painful memories of the day wiped away under the expertise of his killer hands and French whispers, my broken fingers buried in ice.

Now my head was clear.

I tracked the moment of the flat head and flickering tongue, my groin heat seductive to a cold blooded reptile. I cursed at the first flickering inside my penis.

This was not the time for sexual arousal. Space in the sleeping bag was severely restricted, I could not lash out with certainty.

The cold slithering body raised itself onto my abdomen.

As the snake head passed my penis, it stopped, its flickering tongue assessing the throbbing, hard obstacle.

The serpent froze, I froze.

My penis throbbed involuntarily at the delicate stroking of the forked tongue.

With a shift movement I raised my right hand and grabbed the invader by the neck, my left hand flicked the machete and severed the head of the snake from its writhing body.

For a second I felt the hissing from the gaping mouth

blew over my penis.

Like a frightened mouse my manhood shrivelled up from the shock and retreated. I pulled the snake from the sleeping bag and threw it aside.

The next morning the vinegary smell of barbecued snake meat woke me up. The meat tasted like chicken but was easier to chew.

Abel and I spoke little during the day, we focused our energies and strength on keeping up with the little brown pudding creature and his fleeting feet.

On the fourth night Abel and I lay back on our backs gazing at the star curtain.

Abel held my hand in his.

The warmth of the sand heating our backs. Kuyu's silhouette vaguely noticeable on a dune to our right.

He stood on one leg again, gazing into the night in the hope of spotting the fire bubbles from the dragon living in the crack in the earth's crust.

'Kaner?'

'Hmmmm.'

'You sleeping?'

'No dreaming.'

'About what?'

'That.'

'What the moon and the stars?'

'No Wally, heaven.'

'Why? Even if I believed in it, there is no way old Gabriel will allow us in.'

'Why not.'

'Well, we took lives.'

'Only because they tell us to. We defend our country!'

'Is that the only reason? Are you holding other people

responsible? I don't.'

'Kaner, we are not of age yet, do as we are told, our mother signed our papers. Remember the night general arrived with the other three officers. I stood and watched the through the window. They talked a long time, Mother Abishag signed, she did not cry, or was upset. General Venter spent the night at home, the other officers left. My suspicion was Mother Abishag wanted to rid of us herself.'

'He slept with Mother Abishag, well he went into her room anyway, what do you think they did, sign more papers or poured over our files?'

'What!' Abel sat upright. 'That is not possible. How do you know?'

'I sat in the corridor, keeping guard over her room. He sneaked into her room, a small gramophone player in his hand. The sounds of Pohjola's daughter drifted from their room, what do you think they were doing, listening to music?'

'What did you do, did they see you?'

'I went back to my bed. Father was dead, Mother Abishag could do what she wanted. Look! A shooting star. Make a wish Abel!'

'No you must, you saw it first.'

'Ok!'

I pressed my eyes close and wished.

'What did you wish for?'

'I can't tell you.'

'Come on, give me a hint. I am your brother! We share all, we do not have secrets for each other, or do we?'

'Never admit to secrets in your life, remember

grandma Esther always told us, a secret is knowledge only you possess. Essential for one's comfort in life, she said, you always laughed Abel, comfort in life, what does it mean Grandma, you pestered her.'

'She never answered, our Grandma, I do miss her, and the farm, we should go when we have a chance, will you come with me? No shooting of turtle doves, I promise, only cousin Alex. I just wanted to protect you that day, I was jealous, you know.'

'I wish to see the Spider woman again.'

'Oh brother, you can't still believe in that story.'

I jumped up.

'But I do. I was there. Mother Abishag was there. One day I will have to kill you to make her prophecy come true.'

'Why would you want to kill me?'

'I don't know, maybe you hurt me, my destiny, just like the Bible story.'

'Oh you cannot kill me for hurting you, and anyway, you do not believe in the Bible, you are a heathen by your own confession.'

'You may break my heart. Or I may receive instructions to kill you.'

'Who on earth would instruct such a senseless action?'

'I don't know, people I work for! I wish to become a professional assassin.'

Abel jumped up and grabbed my hands.

'No No No! That's wrong.'

'Why? I enjoyed killing Temba, it felt weirdly good, playing god, ending a life, watching the spirit depart, I saw a black scorpion rise up from his body and it crawled along the flaming ceiling. What do you want to become, a farmer, working with uncle Jacob?'

'No, a dominee.'

'Oh god Abel, that's worse than being a killer. I kill and you bury. You can pray for the departed souls of my targets every night.'

'What do you think Mother Abishag would say about you becoming a killer?'

'Well, she signed me up for the training, she hardly has reason to object or be upset.'

'I think she wanted you near the General.'

'Why?'

'Because you look like him.'

'I do?'

'Yes, you do not have black hair like the Du Preez.'

'Well Mother Abishag says accidents happen!'

'Then you certainly are an accident!'

'I have blue eyes.'

'Not like the Du Preez.'

'Well, if I am not Father's child what about you? Father was short.'

'Mother Abishag is tall.'

'Oh I don't know Abel. How can you believe a world adults say. They lie all the time. Do you think we will lie one day?'

'No, I won't you will! I will be a man of God.'

'Oh yes, as if god has never lied to us. And why me? I always get to do the bad stuff? Why am I the son of another man? If Father could hear you now, he may well be up there somewhere, he would have something to say on the matter, or glare at you over his glasses.'

'Yes, but you will be the killer. You can not going

around confessing to your deeds, if someone ask you what you do for a living, so you will have to lie, starting now.'

'Well, I will choose my company wisely so they will know what I do for a living and will have no reason for invading questions.'

'Quiet. Don't move!'

'Why?'

'Snake.'

'Ok Abel, not again, last night shortened my life.'

'Just joking brother!'

We burst out laughing. I wrestled with him in the sand. In the distance Kuyu rolled down the dune, making his way back to us.

## Crunch Time!

The next morning the helicopter was waiting as agreed. Relief washed over us at the sight of the glimmering black whirlybird sitting in the sand basin surrounded by dunes.

I planted a kiss on Abel and Kuyu's lips. Kuyu jumped back in disgraced disgust, I was not sure men pushing their lips together was a custom his tribe indulged in, the otjize ochre mix tasted bitter, I wiped it from my lips.

Kuyu sped ahead from these white boys indulging in bizarre activities. Abel and I laughed, challenging each other, last one at the helicopter is a an old woman with wet panties around her ankles.

To our surprise the general jumped out to welcome us.

His smile disappeared as we expressed our surprise to see him. In black shorts, a T-shirt, trainers and dark sunglasses he looked dressed for a walk down the beach. Kuyu declined the offer of transport.

With his round belly filled with fresh water he set off into the desert, making his way back to the camp under his own steam with a stop at his tribe on the way, to pay his respect to his elders.

The general wasted no time getting on with business. He pulled two brown envelopes from his briefcase minutes after the helicopter rose from the sand.

He face was grave behind the glasses. I glanced at Abel, but his eyes were fixed on the envelopes held out in our direction.

Each envelope stamped top secret between two diagonal red line. On the first page the face of young black man stared at me. Julius Nyere. Somewhere in the back of my mind, a bell rang.

The name was familiar, I'd heard it mentioned in class, maybe around the evening fires. A sharp intake of breath from Abel.

His file slipped out of his hand, the General grabbed it, closed it.

I looked at Abel.

His eyes met mine.

The blood drained from his five day desert tan. The General pressed the file back into Abel's hand. I was not sure if I was mistaken, but it appeared the General was shielding the file from me. I returned my attention to my file.

Julius was 21.

Mission: befriend, infiltrate, extract and terminate.

Julius was a student at the Witwatersrand University, an outspoken youth, suspected of close ties with the

Russians, introducer of infiltrates to the highly impressionable student society. He made inroads into the newspapers, the lefties, opposition of the Pretoria government. Newspaper articles flashed back.

'A thorn in our flesh,' the general said, 'not painful at the moment, an uncomfortable itch, a lesion with the potential to suppurate. We can not quite afford his disappearance in JB.'

JB stood for Jackie Brown, a downtown police station in City of Gold, facist detention bastion, here one slip, whether on the stairs, a banana skin or bar of soap, can be fatal. The general told anecdotes of men, so desperate for an escape from the relentless interrogation, they jumped from windows, they threw themselves at death.

'We need your imagination, skill and youth Kaner, get rid of him. Check his resources, he arranges safe passage for international terrorists. He is slippery, his infamous chants of kill the farmer tarnish our international negotiations, give him a dose of his own medicine, who the hell does this man think he is? Leader of renegade impis? Get rid of him. Quickly, I do not care for infiltration. Just do it. We can have no man call for the killing of our own people on the public stage. Take him out.'

The general waved his hand in the air like he was swatting a fly. I wondered why he wore his black leather gloves, in this heat and with shorts, but he always did when handling the secret files, never touching the files with his naked hands.

I paged through, photos of Julius filled the file, notes on his likes and dislikes, he was a guitar player, flamenco lover, photos of a young leader at a illegal student rallies with a raised AK47 above his head, sweeping up the youth masses. I stopped reading with a shock, place of birth: Lambutshashi. Scorpion Boy, Fezela Boy.

I looked at the general.

He nodded.

'Yes, they grew up together. The elders sponsored higher education for Julius, seeing potential in him as a leader, he lost the plot, his funding is now undertaken by the Commies.'

I looked up at Abel.

His eyes still focused on page one. He stroked the photo of his target.

The look on his face intrigued me. The general removed the files from our hands, placed them back in the briefcase and told us to place the headphones over our heads.

Classical music played. The general rested his head back with his eyes closed and one gloved hand on Abel's leg.

I did not recognise the piece, but was in no doubt it was Sibelius. The general opened one eye, an eye watching me closely. I raised my shoulder.

'What is this music?' I asked, pointing at the headphones.

'Rakastava, a man like no other man, a lover, a companion, listen carefully for the weary traveller getting home to his warm cabin in the rimy wasteland of the north, resting his head against the wooden door as he closed it firmly behind him after the endless journey hunting bears for food in the hostile world of the Finnish winters. Get yourself to Finland one day Kaner, you and Abel, and you will understand the soul of the killer, the assassin, for there man is in constant battle with nature and the other life forms. I survived three months in the middle of winter, armed with only a knife when I was your age. You will revel in the susurrus of the streams in the spring, life coming alive, you are fond of nature, the dead of winter replaced by the buoyancy of spring. Training was very different in those days, you boys have it easy nowadays.'

The general looked away, reverie sweeping his mind from the present.

I looked down, the dunes swept by, the wasteland of Africa, an epic world so opposite from the north.

I decided that one day I would visit Finland, the images in my head conjured up a world of snow, imaginary creatures and people walking around in long fox and mink coats.

Brave people killing with their hands, not because the bald men with black suits and round glasses told them to do so, but to survive, eat and burn energy.

I could see Abel and me living in a hut in the middle of frozen forests with our mother, we would hunt in the day and at night, we would sit down around the fire and tell fables of times long gone.

The happy feeling of seeing home filled me as the familiar buildings of Camp Basawa appeared in the distance.

The last notes disappeared quietly, as if the weary traveller closed the door behind him. For a brief moment I wondered what it feels like to be a lover and a traveller.

Always resting your head against the person you love and travel with, never coming to rest in one place.

The desire burned inside me like the desert furnace

heat to see the world, what lay beyond the horizon of this endless desert and the blue skyline, what is the world like where the sky and earth meet, do they ever?

# A lion and three warthogs

There

are nights in your life you always remember, and
then there are nights like this one......when you scream
and laugh at your company, even if they were not a
Catfish or the Bottlemen type.

Abel and I joined the General around the fire for
dinner. We turned down his offer of a brandy, it was best
to keep our heads clear. The moment a file landed in our
laps the countdown began.

Conversation was sparse, the General asked about
our time in the desert, we responded with little detail. I
sensed my brother was not on board with us. Abel was
simmering, what about I was not sure, we had not had
time since we landed for conversation.

I showered and read on the bed, trying keeping my

mind off Julius, but the news that he was from the same village as Bokero Bazuli intrigued me.

Mama told us on this planet we are all connected and related to each other, would I be able to ask Julius about Bokero, what he was like as a little boy, how did he get the butterfly cloak? The human chain Mama called it, we are all linked, she said with a sad smile. Abel kept busy in his barracks. I braaied the meat and we ate without saying much. An eerie silence hung over the desert, as if the desert animals were recovering from their festive celebrations. I wondered where Kuyu was, did he asleep alone under the stars, nestling his body into a cavity in the sand, radiating heat for the sand creatures?

'Kaner, tell us a a bedtime story,' the general said, 'but not one of your fantasy stories, something real, damn it. You should live in the real world, like a soldier, we soldiers do not have time for airy fairy stories.' He slurred his words, one look at the brandy bottle informed me the general had already started his end of year celebrations. Something he was most probably entitled to. Who did he spent Christmas with - I was not even sure if the general had family. A thought shot through me, Mama perhaps, but I wiped the thought from my mind. I leaned back against a dried tree stump, looking up at the sky, my mind racing through the events of the last days in the desert, trying to make enough connections to form a story.

'Don't entertain the bastard,' Abel said, his voice hoarse. I looked up at him. His eyes were fixed on the General who shifted upright in his chair.

'Hey Soldier, what is with you, who kicked sand into your eyes, a little dung beetle perhaps, you better watch your.......' Abel did not allow the General to finish his sentence.

'Or else what? You will order the compilation of another brown top secret file, this time perhaps with my photo on the front? Who will you entrust with my killing? My brother? Lieutenant Herholdt? Or will you undertake the honour yourself? And how will you keep it top secret, oh boys, you should do not discuss your targets.' Abel imitated the general's speech in a comical way. I half sniggered, not quite sure where the conversation was going, what was the matter with Abel, heat stroke perhaps? He certainly was lifting the lid off his simmering mood. I tried to remember what Father Isaac said about a bee under a bonnet. I straightened up, just in case a restraining order was barked by the General. I noticed he glanced over his shoulders in the direction of the guards at the gate. Abel stood up and lifted a smouldering stump from the fire, he waved it through the air, sparks flew everywhere. He waved the burning stump in front of the General. The General did not flinch.

'Abel, sit down, what is wrong with you?' I hoped my voice would calm my brother. He swung around in my direction. The smouldering stump held in front of him like a spear.

'It's Alex, cousin Alex, the man you lost your childhood virginity to.'

I did not register, my mind flushed with past and present images. I looked at him, I looked at the General.

'What do you mean?'

'Which part did you not understand my dearest brother?' Abel swayed on his feet. I scrutinised his face, his pupils blown, dilated, he was under blue vial influence, did he steal or save a vile, we were suppose to hand all vials back.

'The man who fucked you the night our grandfather died, remember, I stood there watching you giving yourself to our cousin, like a cheap whore, was that your way of expressing your hatred for our father, spitting on his grave, or were you getting back at me for killing the innocent dove when you and your lover-to-be swam in the dam? Did you set out to seduce him, like you set out to seduce me, standing over my bed each night, stroking my body, hardly able to contain your breathing, did you really think I was asleep all the time? My dear freakish little brother who always lived in my shadow.' I rose from my chair and stood tall, attempting a futile staring down of my brother. Despite the sweltering night temperatures, a chill ran down my spine as I stared into the cold entrancing blue eyes of my brother. With a jolt I realised I looked into the eyes of a killer. Right now, right here, Abel was in a state to clasp his hands over my throat and force the last breath of life from my lungs. What would I do, kill back? Was this the moment? I looked at the general. He leaned back in his chair, his arms folded behind his head, was he enjoying this little scene? Happy the attention was detracted from him? I tilted my head slightly to the left, pondering whether to take my brother out with a left hook. Something stopped me, it was clear to me Abel was not himself, but I sensed he had something to get off his chest.

'It's cousin Alex, I have to kill cousin Alex,' he murmured. I looked at the general.

'Why?' I asked. Have the bald men on the radio gone mad or was I possibly the one with sunstroke? The general slowly raised from his chair and walked over to us, he towered above us.

'You are all sick, the whole lot of you Du Preez's. My
god, your grandfather would turn in his grave if he
caught sight of you lot now. How the fuck did you lot
manage to carry the family name of Du Preez? And you
two, you two who own part of one of the most
respectable farms in this country decided to give
yourself to each other in the back of a submarine. My
god, what have I created, two little rampant locusts
humping each other from behind. And you my little
Kaner boy, child of Poprygunya, acting like a blood
thirsty praying mantis, devouring your mating partner,
don't look so shocked, you are in the company of men,
no secrets between the three of us. I do not need a brown
file, here we are, I rescued you two from the idle life you
were destined to live in that wretched town of Peaceful
Glen, squandering your waking hours with idle dreams
and fantasies, I am the ant and you two are the
grasshoppers. This country does not stand a fucking
hope in hell with you lot.'

Abel and I were caught off guard. We'd never referred
to the night after the killing of Bokero, we arrived back
in the camp and went our separate ways. I should have
guessed nothing escaped the attention of the Boss, we
were at the end of the day, his most precious creations,
the man who never spoke of love, women or his private
life. I touched the leg of my brother, in the hope of
distracting him. Abel did not look at me. He and the
general locked eyes, the bull and the matador, red flag
waved. The look on the General's face spoke volumes.
Was it fear, or the realisation he left the cat out of the
bag? Rank fell to the wayside as Abel stretched up to his
full height, now towering over the General by a few
centimetres. A young fighter against an old, experienced

112

warrior. Silence descended around us, broken occasionally by the crack of burning wood sparked up in flames. In the distance the old lion roared, his voice trembling across the desolate land, saying goodbye to the old year. Abel reached out, his right hand hovered in front of the general, it took all his willpower not to grab the General by the throat. Abel lowered his hand and when he spoke it was in a low voice. I strained my ears to catch his words.

'You will keep your mouth shut over my brother and I, never would you say another word of what transpired between us, for your Bolshevistic mind is limited in its thinking, I have done my homework too dearest general, I move faster through the night than an old dog with creaking joints like you can ever dream of moving. When your time is up, I will steal through the dark hours of the night, carrying out secret missions, I can crush you now, what are you going to do? Call on your guards? Who will come to your rescue old bull, you are nothing without your puny stars and castles on your shoulders. You trained us, the best in the world, now sit back and enjoy the bit of power you still have, writing files, sticking photos on. I will crush you, like a crocodile crushes the head of an antelope if you so much as say another word about my mother. Whatever transpired between the two of you in the past, I do not care. You will never understand my brother and I, we are Du Preez men, my father was and so was my grandfather, men who worked this earth hard and honestly, so do not make reference to us again, even in a moment of anger or jest.' The General and Abel faced each other, arms dropped at their side, but tensed, ready for action.

'I made you, you and your brother are my creations,

whether you are comfortable with that notion or not, I am not interested. I can destroy you, your youth doesn't count for much in my books. You sleep sound at night, don't you? I am the one hovering over you, measuring your heartbeat, watching you holding your brother's hand in the moonlight on the dune, that was touching. I give it to you boys, the snake in the sleeping bag, well done to your brother. Next time you two may not wake-up, so watch your mouth young man. This year is coming to an end and you have not been able to cling onto your mother's apron strings for twenty four months, I will tear the score card up tonight, wipe the slate clean and let you dump whatever you carried on your chest into the fire. But you listen to me, with great care, I crush fleas between my eye lashes without so much as a blink. I will have no hesitation in suspending my guardianship of you and your brother, one word from me into the international network and you two become open season targets, there will be no safe house for you, our friends in the ANC, SWAPO, KGB, Chinese Secret Service will be keen to learn who destroyed their cosy killer camps and trained agents. Do I make myself clear trooper Du Preez?

'You know General, my Mama taught us a man who threatens is a man not coping well with his own insecurities.'

'And your Mama, if I am not mistaken, also said a drunk man does not make false promises. Your mind is wide open now, I noticed from the size of your pupils, it is always good to know where one stands with one's squad.'

Abel raised his right hand, I expected the worse, but he saluted the general with a flick of his head to the right and walked off into the night. So unaware of his beastly sexuality he stalked off with the agility of a black panther. The General walked over to his chair and emptied the remains of the brandy bottle down his throat. The empty bottle he threw into the fire, he shot a glance in my direction with a look I did not care to analyse, before he stomped off in the direction of this house, his shoulders slumped.

I remained seated, starring at the embers of the fire, the night sky filled with the smell of the burned out wood. I was not sure what to make of it all, the accusations, the clash of male wills, the overspill of aggression, would everything be the way it was in the morning? Wills had clashed and for a moment I feared the casting vote would rest with me to decide who I wanted as my leader.

# Convocation

I stepped outside the barracks and walked over to the laboratory.

With a hair pin I picked the lock and entered.

Rows of laboratory gear stood cleaned, waiting to be used by the young white scientific brains of the country, at the moment sunning themselves somewhere on a beach or enjoying the fine bakes and holiday pastries of their mothers, washed down with homemade ginger beer.

I walked past the benches. In the furthest corner was the office of the head technician. The door was not locked. I sniggered at the ease of my trespassing.

I headed for the large inbuilt fridge behind his desk. The air was thick, stale with some of the planet's most extreme noxious and lethal concoctions. If ever there was a viper's nest, this was it.

Poisonous snakes, spiders and scorpions bred and bio-engineered for their toxic powers.

The air was still, death does not move, not fast anyway, it lurked in waiting, keeping out of human sight. Six drawers in the fridge.

Drawer five labelled Abel/Karelia. How I hated uneven numbers, my request for number six ignored, stupid laboratory technicians, coldblooded reptiles, never seeing the sun.

I pulled the drawer open. Rows of cobalt blue vials greeted me.

I took six and pushed them into the backpack. From the laboratory I headed for the general's office. To my surprise the office was occupied.

The Boss sat in a chair by the window, the curtains drawn, a sunlight sliver shone onto the table.

He smoked a cigar, dark glasses covered his eyes, his hair damp and combed, a bottle of Cognac on the side table. He waved me in, I stepped forward.

'Kaner, Happy New Year Son, may this be one of the fucking best years of your life, and your brother, and certainly mine, for who the hell knows, this maybe the last time we are granted the opportunity to wish each other Happy New Year.'

I closed the door behind me, treading with caution. My appetite for conflict gone.

'Going anywhere for New Year's day, somewhere sunny, or cold, Finland? Or is there a more sinister reason you are not in bed, but in my office, at eight o'clock in the morning on New Year's day. Did you know I never locked my office?'

I shook my head.

His attempt at humour filled me with vile horror.

The slunk hero was gone, the shoulders were straightened, with the aid of cognac, a cigar and dark glasses the old bastard was ready for another battle.

Why did he not heed Abel's warning?

What would happen if I killed him now?

Who would know, would he squirm?

He deserved to take his big mouth six feet under the ground with him. I saluted the old dog, he was in uniform, and placed the rucksack on the floor.

He raised his right hand, returning my show of respect in a half hearted manner.

It did not matter.

'I am reporting for duty Sir, I am ready to take my leave and commence duty.' I pointed at the red folders, on the floor, at his feet, the folders Abel and I held on our laps in the helicopter.

He looked down at the folders, at me and then at the bottle. He filled his glass and drank from it. His head in a halo of exhaled cigar smoke.

He bent forward and placed the folders onto his lap.

'Which one?'

'What do you mean General, I thought you wanted-'

He cut me short.

'I did not train you to think Kaner, only to do as I say.' I nodded.

'Yes Sir, do you mean I have a choice?'

'One always have choices in life, Son. You have the choice of target, whose life will you terminate, which enemy of your country will you send on his way, long before they played out the last chapter of their lives?'

I was confused. He noticed.

He stood up and stepped closer to me. He rested his right hand on my shoulder, the left hand held the glass. His breath stale, I slowed my breathing so as not to inhale his scavenger breath.

'In life we are the authors of our own stories, everyday we write another chapter, but men like you and I play god over the chapters in others people's live, we decide when they run out of ink, when their pens dry up and they have nothing left to write on the empty pages of their lives, for in the story of our lives, our targets are mere side characters,  we are empowered by the state, our enemies' last chapter is another chapter in the trilogy of our lives, but.....'

He circled around me glass in hand.

Would he be surprised if I reach for the backpack and filled a syringe with liquid. Would he suspect my desire to terminate his life, finish off his hold over Abel and I, the secret keeper, the man with the power to keep us apart?

He was stronger than me, I did not doubt it for a moment, but I was young, I was a cub, he was an old lion, I could outmanoeuvre him.

The Boss halted on my left side and tapped with his middle finger against my temple. A nicotine stench drifted up my nostrils.

I concentrated on not swallowing, the emotional and physical link between thought and the movement drilled into our heads by our Israeli instructions, the masters of body language.

From behind his dark glasses the General studied my every movement, his penetrating glaze searching for signals revealing my brain patterns.

I did not flinch, my eyes focused on the yellow slither of sunlight. The dust fairies riding up and down.

He turned away, walked over to the folders, picked them up and held them in front of me.

Operation Triangle Sun.

Operation Miracle of Love.

'Take your pick, play God Kaner. Your choice. What better death can man ask for, but to drink from nature's sweet nectar offered by the hand of an innocent child, for that is all you are, my son, a child, you see life ebb and flow, but you have seen so little of life itself.'

He invited me to sit down on the chair in front of the desk. The General walked around the desk, sat down in the leather chair, he put his feet on the desk and folded his hands pyramid style in front of his chin, studying me, wondering, like I wondered about him.

The chair creaked as he leaned forward, his stomach folded, it was the first time I noticed the excess weight on the man I admired and hated in equal measures, I was not quite sure why, but I did.

He opened the cupboard door behind his desk and placed six vials in front of me, it contained a dark yellow liquid, much darker than the vials in my backpack.

'Specially developed for you, boosted Egyptian cobra poison added to your standard mixture. My New Year's gift to you. Make sure you apply within 30 days, beyond the expiry date death is not guaranteed.' He smirked. 'It never is anyway.'

I held the vials in front of my eyes, studying the look of poison, natural death, not death by my hand, Gods', nature, a fellow life form.

'You are different from the others, I see young men like you pass through this camp year after year, every one desperate to find himself, to prove himself, but you, you somehow have a confidence at odds with the youth of your years.'

The man did not make sense to me, I nodded a respectful 'yes I understand.'

'You know you will never have children,' he said after taking a big swirl from the glass.

'I never think of it.'

'One day you will, oh yes you will.' His voice tinged with an emotion unknown to me. 'And when you do, nature will raise her middle fingers at you.' The General pushed both folders next to the vials.

'Time to choose Kaner. It's only a name of a story, which one do you want to read, which one do you want to be part of? You are in a book store, your finger trail over the titles, it stops on the Triangle Sun, next to it you read the title Miracle of Love. Your imagination is invoked, the little voice in your mind whispers a story to you, is it a story of lovers sleeping tight, holding onto each others bodies, breathing warm breath over each other? Where are you Kaner, are you in bed or are you standing next to the bed, watching, waiting for the moment, as you listen to the music, the beautiful haunting sounds of the Karelia Overture drifts into your mind.'

The air was stale.

I took a deep breath, touching my Adam's apple. His voice was low, a whisper.

'Karelia kill, kill, kill, now.'

I looked into the pale blue eyes, the sun glasses

121

resting on the folders.

Like a frightening mouse hypnotised by an angry defensive cobra, I had no will, my will belonged to the eyes, the hypnotic swaying of him, larger than me, I subjected myself to his will, his wish my command, I was not in charge, I awaited his instruction, he was the story master, guiding me in the composition of my life.

The General placed the vials on the folders and pushed both across the desk in my direction, along with the sunglasses.

'Julius, my assignment,' I said and pointed at the red folder.

He stared at me. He leaned back in the black leather recliner chair.

He reached out for the folder, and paged through it before handing it to me.

'You surprise me Kaner.'

'Why is that General,' I asked as I reached for the red folder.

We both held onto it from opposite ends. His breath was sweet, stale, seductive. For a moment a thought shot through my head, what if, what if I strip naked, now, would this man be able to resist my firm body.

Abel had told me on the submarine the morning after our first assignment, when I woke up and found him propped up on one elbow, stroking and caressing my body, 'You are beautiful brother, your body has changed, you are a man now.'

I starred at him in disbelief, was it true, because when I looked in the mirror, all I saw was a skinny young man, firm in places, but by all means not an Adonis.

'But my eyes, they can never be beautiful, slits like a

Siamese cat. Look at your beautiful eyes brother, why can't I have beautiful eyes like you?'

Abel smiled pussycat style before he pushed my head into the raven black forest sprouting abundantly above his groin, obliterating further words.

I shook my head to clear it.

'You okay?' the General asked.

I nodded a yes.

I stepped forward and took the Operation Sun Triangle folder.

I pushed the substantial thick file into the rucksack.

'I need transport General, to at least Windhoek, I will get a train from there to City of Gold, I would like to pass by Peaceful Glen and greet Mother Abishag and my sister, I have never seen her.'

I felt excitement at the mention of the women in my life, one I had yet to rest my eyes on.

The General opened the drawer and pulled an envelope out.

'Two thousand rand,' he said, 'spend wisely, your papers are in the folder, you are a student from the moment you leave the camp. Emergency numbers and contact names are in the folder, destroy the folder once the detail is memorised.'

His hand disappeared into the drawer again, he lifted a 9mm out.

I shook my head.

'Take it, come back in 30 days and tell me all son. Go forth soldier, terminate the enemies of the state, so your mother, sister and brother can sleep safe at night. The guards will drive you to Windhoek, read the folder on your way, memorise the detail, you cannot take the paperwork with you, only the faces, names, details and titles.'

We both stood up.

He hugged me, kissed me on the forehead.

I stood back, saluted him, and left the room with my backpack, folders and twelve vials of poison.

As I reached the door, the General called me back, he held out six blue bottles filled with the magical brown liquid, this time each bottle was in a red leather pouch embroidered with a black scorpion.

The black scorpion signature range expanded. I put the sunglasses on.

'And try to get a decent haircut in the city, the soft city souls may think I have send them Tarzan reincarnated.' His boisterous laughter bounced over the camp.

Outside one of the guards waved me in the direction of the jeep.

A thin trail of white smoke drifted up from the kitchen chimney, fried bacon smells wafting into the sky, New Year's day breakfast.

The General stood on the verandah, signalling the engine to be started. Abel stood in the doorway of the barracks. I asked the driver to stop and jumped out.

'Morning, happy New Year brother,' he said and kissed me on both cheeks.

I kissed him on the lips knowing the General was watching.

'It's time,' I said.

'You are not waiting for me?' I shook my head.

'How long will you be?'

I shrugged. My brother looked over my shoulder, I

turned around, following his gaze, it focused on the folder poking from the bag on the passenger seat.

Abel grabbed me by the shoulders and spun me around. A question mark suspended on his face.

'Life is about choices,' I said, 'ask for a different assignment, I can take care of the family affairs afterwards, its my debt to repay, give me ten days, its all I need, I am going to see Mother Abishag and Penny-Pitstop first.'

'Are you sure?'

'Yes.'

We hugged.

I climbed back into the jeep and did not look back as we drove through the cross bowed elephant tusks above the gate. The heat was building up and I was grateful for the sunglasses.

It was a long drive, my mind raced back over the last twenty fours months since our arrival at Camp Basawa.

How much had happened in two years. Abel and I knew little what to expect, boys we were, boys with no hair on the station, well at least I had none, now I had.

I had made love to my brother, I had killed a handicapped killer, I had slept with my instructors, the finest men in the world, the most dangerous, fearless men.

What next, what next awaits me, only time will tell, as the General said, I have to write chapters, until another writer sails over the open window of my bedroom, catching me by surprise or in my sleep and put a full stop after my next breath.

I was aware I was too young to think of death at such an early age, but death had entered my life, long before I was ready to receive it.

I made peace with the looming shadow, for what is there to fear of death, but death itself. The old lion had reenergised himself on death, new life breathed into him by feasting on the remains of life. I leaned back against the headrest of the seat.

The arid landscape, my eyes scanning the horizon. Since I watched the old lion-man disappear into the sea, I had not been able to rid myself of the feeling of fearful apprehension, a sense of foreboding.

Out there an unknown spirit awaited me, unseen eyes watching me, the eyes of restless souls. I scanned the dunes, is she there, the old lady with the grey hair, watching me, waiting to spin her web of evil so the spell she cast on me can be fulfilled?

What chance did I stand against the united force of a spider witch and a scorpion soldier?

I looked up, high above in the sky a lonely lightning bird flew, it squawked a lonely call, did Kuyu not point out the day in the desert when a hammerkop fly over you, it was a sign of someone close has died or is about to die?

Kuyo was so filled with fear and anxiety, he fell down on his knees and began clicking in IXam, the ancient San language of Africa, a language he later told us the spirits of his great-grandfathers taught him in his sleep.

All children spoke the same language many moons ago, he believed, a time when Africa lived in fabled glory of kings and queens ruling over the delicate people of Africa.

The fear on his face chilled my heart as I sat here, on the first day of a new year, watching the messenger of

126

death flying hight above in the open skies.

## *My mother! Oh my mother!*

'Welcome to Peaceful Glen,' the station board read, 'the penultimate stop on this track, alight now or stay onboard until the end.'

I arrived back home two days later than expected. Engine problems left us stranded in the ghost village of Aus.

I spent two nights sleeping under the black cape of stars in one of the brick building ruins built by the German inmates during the First World War interment.

From there I caught a ride on an old mailing train. I sat in the guards van with the signalman.

A funny old man he was with most of his teeth missing. He offered me stale sandwiches soaked in melting Marmite. He loved his trains and entertained me all the way with tales.

A few times the steam engine with its stopped in the middle of nowhere. The fireman, machinist and signalman taking time out to enjoy a cup of strong black coffee and rusks in the shade of a lonely tree.

We passed through the loneliest towns I ever saw, many with only one single street. When I passed comment the signalman joked, 'there is only one pick-up in this town.'

The slow snail pace train journey afforded me the chance of seeing the extraordinary beauty of a part of country I never saw.

My thoughts drifted to him I thought was my Father, but now seemed was not. A traveller and gypsy he was at heart. In his grey Zephyr he crossed the vast and sparsely populated expanses of our lands, selling household wares like white candles, pots and pans, newspapers, primus stoves and paraffin.

Back home, as we laid on the lawn feasting on water melon slices, he promised one day he'd take us away from Peaceful Glen. Wide eyed Abel and I listened. 'We will criss-cross the deserts of our land, travel through forests stuffed with roaming elephants and roaring lions.'

I sniggered at the memory I accepted as a truth of my past. Now it seemed to me more like a falsehood.

The signalman asked me what was wrong with my face. I shook my head and took a sip of the brandy flask he held out. Here and there decrepit trekboer farmhouses with leaky looking thatch stood desolately lonely in the veld.

In the door of a few of these derelict houses stood a coloured woman with a child on the hip. An excitement welled up in me. Soon I will see Dinah again. If I were to be honest, I probably looked forward to seeing her more than my own mother, the deceitful Jezebel.

Now and then the steam engines grounded noisily to a halt to pick up nothing more than a solitary milk churn.

Rickety look screw pile bridge structures helped the train crossed dried river beds from long dry spells. The long days and hours passed by. I welcomed the solitude and the chance to sort my thoughts.

It was a clear afternoon the steam engine puffed into Peaceful Glen station. The station deserted of human life. From the station I walked up the hill with the bag slung over my shoulder.

My too tight shorts chaffed my thighs.

It felt strange.

I no longer was the little scrawny schoolboy following Abel back from the school across the trail tracks and up the hill to where the two bedroom house still stood forlorn.

The front gates stood open and hung loose from a rusted hinge. Weeds replaced the grass carpet where Mother Abishag directed magical stories from the sky when we were little boys.

The weeds were in full bloom. In their wildness they infested and strangled the rose buses.

The absence of the hand of man was evident everywhere. A brown child with long and narrow eyes like mine played under the fig tree. She looked up and smiled the moment she caught sight of me.

I waved at her. 'Amara, is that you?'

She gazed back with a stupid blank look in her eyes. A piece of green snot slugged from her nose.

She poked her finger in and stuck the slimy finger into her mouth, then she licked it.

I decided not to kiss her. I looked around but saw no sign of Dinah. I could not help but to smile thinking how silly Abel and I were.

We thought Father slept with Dinah and she expected our half-brother. When Father so suddenly died in the car crash, all hell broke loose during the will reading. Everyone, including Grandma Esther thought Father fathered a bastard child.

How could I forgot the relief look on the face of Mother Abishag when she saw Dina gave birth to an all brown baby girl and not to a bastard son.

Washing flapped in the breeze. The scene in front of me was all so familiar, but with a strangeness I could not place my finger on. Almost two years passed since Abel and I walked from this yard for the long drive to Camp Basawa.

Time passed.

Somewhere along the line my childhood passed too. I was not even sure I still belonged here.

Old affections streamed back the moment I saw my old beloved fig tree standing forlorn. Its branches faithfully still stroking the window of the bedroom where Abel and I spent our school years.

I could not wait to climb in and one more time escape from the world. Up in the tree nothing ever mattered.

The kitchen door stood open. With apprehension I stepped inside that room where Father lost his temper so badly with me in the weeks before he died in the car accident.

I shivered.

With relief I noticed at least the kitchen was spotless clean. The sun still bounced gleamingly off the polished wooden floor.

Black and white designs painted on the walls and floor. Pockets of light and darkness. Innocence and guilt. The tall dark shadow of my presence cast onto the kitchen floor as a shaded part of a picture of domestic bliss.

I no longer felt part of this picture for a simple reason. On dark new moon Monday morning Mother Abishag took my hand and walked me away from this little house on top of the hill.

I could not hope, nor dared I pray, to become part of this family life again.

Well at least not until the repair work was completed to the swallow nest roof, the burst clay walls and the floorboards.

I listened.

But no, even the ants in labyrinths yonder the floorboards held their breaths for my arrival. There was not shrieking joyously celebrating the return of the killer son.

'Hello,' I called into the house.

A shock silence reached out. Did Mother Abishag enjoyed a nap? The sound of little feet running up the hallway floor reached my ear.

A tiny voice shrieked, 'Whose there?'

Then this little thing stepped from a hallway shadow.

The same spot where I sat that night watching the shadow of my father flowed across from the guest bedroom into the marital bedroom.

A thin ray of sun falling through the small swing framed window gently stroked her curly blonde hair, then seeped into her sky blue innocent eyes.

Her skin, golden brown. A little butterfly, sorrow unburdened.

Dressed in black and white she stood eyeing me cautiously, like a crow checking out a snare.

It was clear to me little baby girl knew not what to make of the stranger in the kitchen door. A tiny fat finger she sucked on.

Oh boy, what a little impulsive cupcake delight.I just knew it was Mara - the fruit from the loins of our heavily pregnant Mother Abishag.

I kneeled down. I held my arms open.

So much for being a cold blooded killer.

By God, I was keenly interested in this little one. Tiptoeing with cautious hesitation she stepped forward. In her eyes I read her desire of instinctive trust.

She wanted to trust me, her instincts told her it was okay to trust this stranger in the kitchen.

'Hey, you must be Mara. I am your brother, Kaner,' I whispered to her, gently so as not to frighten her, no different from speaking to a young gazelle.

She smelled of baby powder.

I nuzzled my nose into her neck, inhaling the innocent childhood short-lived fragrance.

On her soft puckered baby lips I planted a kiss. Tiny fat fingers stroked my hair, my beard.

An unknown tenderness welled up from a source deep inside of me.

I pressed her podgy baby body against mine.

For a brief moment she stood still, then wriggled

freed. 'You will never have children Kaner,' the haunting little voice inside of me called out.

From the dark corridor her all too familiar voice shut my inner voice up.

'Well, well, well,' she said. I looked up. I saw her outline.

'Mother Abishag,' I asked.

'Oh yah, whose asking,' she said.

'Kaner,' I replied.

'Huh, anything may happen on my front door step,' she said from the shadows, 'I thought they locked you up for good in the desert.'

'Take it easy,' I said, momentarily lost for words listening to her train of speech.

'So I have done for some time since you boys deserted your dear mother.'

'We did no such thing,' I said.

Her silence greeted me. I watched the child grabbed an ant from the floor and put into her mouth.

I stepped forward to snatch it from her mouth. Just then the shadow stepped forth, her feet falling with a thud on the floor. We simultaneously grabbed at the child.

'Let go,' said Mother Abishag with a slow smile.

I gasped the moment I witnessed her harsh features.

Dark doubt shadows sat under her eyes. Eyes filled with an insanely light, the tender dreaminess gone.

I stared into them with disbelief. I felt my mouth twisted with distaste seeing her former red candy lips now cracked. There she stood, almost unrecognisable. I controlled my breath.

'Mother Abishag,' I said.

'Mara, your sister,' her all too familiar voice spoke from the corridor.

The sight of her filled with me horror. Was this was I so looked forward to returned to. She let go of herself.

'Mother Abishag.' A dry smile broke over her face. She said nothing in reply.

When she held her arms out I stepped slowly forward.

She smelled of green soap. The same soap Dina used to wash our clothes on the wash plank.

Mother held me at arms length. With her chuffed hands she turned me hands over and over, tracing the fine hairs and palm lines of my hands with her fingers.

Her nails were chipped and colourless and not clean. In stupefied silence we stood marvelling at each other face to face.

I felt the warmth of her breasts, and the warmth of her hands on my face.

For a moment I closed my eyes, reliving childhood memories.

Through the open window I heard the birds in the trees. I wanted this to be a magical moment, but, inside me something slowly altered into a monster.

'Oh my little darling, it feels like years since you stood here. Look at you. You are a man, no longer my little boy.'

Her fingers traced my face, a saddened look came over her face.

'Now all will be alright, the sun is back in my life. Ne me quitte pas, never again my child of the wind will I let go of you. What was I thinking sending my sons away from me. Where is Abel?'

I shook my head, 'He did not come with.' Her eyes pleaded for an answer, but two tiny hands preyed us apart. I did not expect sadness from her.

'How many times did I not think of you two. My days and nights stretched endless ahead of me. If I were not for your little sister.'

I wanted her to finish her sentence.

'Sometimes I felt like my lives with you two never happened. I so hope my Abel will come and pay his respects to me very soon.' Strangely I felt in no mood to tell her anything. She did not ask, did not pry. This is the last time, I kept telling myself.

'Would you like a cup of coffee,' she asked.

Then she busied herself in front of the stove bring the black kettle to the boil. I sat and looked at her. I was not quite sure I missed this all.

In that moment I doubt my well intended visiting intention. On the stove plates she made toast for us. She told me Dina went into town and would be home soon.

We spent our time drinking coffee and eating toast on a blanket spread over the weeds under the fig tree.

I heard bits and bobs of her sentences: 'The birth was difficult....money is scarce....no news from the farm.....my life is my life....your sister keep me sane....no one came to visit anymore...I have not friends left.'

She kept the conversation up, I admired her for that. I could not. The few times I mentioned life in the camp, I noticed she casted her eye all too frequent down and withdrew into silences she did not return from. During those silences I did my best not to stare at her haggardness. Detaching myself from rumpled mess was

136

made easier by her unkept appearances.

'What is he like now,' she said suddenly out of the blue.

I raised an eyebrow then decided to test her.

'My father?'

'What do you mean?'

'Is that not who you meant,' I said.

I carefully observed her eyes, this was the right time to settle a number of things. I wanted her to force into a confession. Once again she paused conversation by gazing down.

'It was obvious, he said nothing, the General that is.'

I noticed she turned pale.

'Look at me,' I said. I tried to hide the expression in my eye, but could not stop mocking her with my eyes.

'You lied to me, made me believe your husband was my father. You stood there in that goddammit kitchen and you let him beat the living day lights out of me over a pair of red underpants. How could you, Mother.'

## *What now my mother!*

Against my wishes I spat the last word out. I felt a rage
reared its ugly angry head inside of me like the adder in
the desert put on guard in his fight with the scorpion. I
cursed myself for being caught off guard. I never
intended raising the topic of who was my father.

She looked up and met my eyes with her calm eyes.

'You hate me,' she said with a serene voice, then
leaned forward and grasped my arm, 'take pity on me, I
was young, I had no choice.'

'No choice!'

I choked on the words. I was indignant. How very
dared she.

'You deceived your family. You made me lead a false
life,' I shouted.

Her eyes filled with sadness. That infuriated me.

'You are not going to open your waterworks on me,

138

are you now Mother,' I shouted. When she spoke again, she lowered her voice.

'I did what I had to do. If I did not, you would not be sitting in front of me now, don't you understand.' I sat still for a moment.

'Why,' I asked at last.

'That is husband and wife stuff. In answer to your question, my husband did not know the two boys he raised was not his. He suspected, but I don't think he really cared. He had his other life.'

'Other life?'

'You know, his travelling sales road show. His other women. He married me for convenience and for nothing else.' She stopped for a long moment.

'What do you mean, nothing else?'

She shook her head, and said, 'That's history bearing no relevance.'

'I will decide what bears relevance,' I said in a rage.

She smiled and her eyes softened even more. When she spoke her voice was hard, 'Don't forget your place. This still is my house and you are my son. You can leave if you so wish.' I was furious.

'You signed away your motherhood claims.'

'A signature on paper, nothing more,' she commented coldly.

I sprang to my feet.

'Then I leave.'

'Why?' I noticed the smile on her face.

'Why you smiling,' I asked.

'You are so like him, you posses his angry naïveté. Looked at your pose. You are his child.'

Mother Abishag fell back on the blanket with her legs

kicking high in the air. I noticed the soft golden hairs covering her bleach white legs.

'What are you doing? I asked, astonished.

'He carried cream coloured leather wine bag the day I met him down there in the sunflower fields. He told me he bought in a small town outside Pamplona. Goat skin, I believe. Have you seen it?'

I shook my head, 'Can't say I have. He never invited me into his personal quarters.'

I doubted she heard me. A dazed look appeared in her veiled eyes.

'There he stood, his biceps strained against the tight sleeves of his T-shirt. I held my breath. I could not believe my eyes. Such a magnificent youthful specimen against a backdrop of sunflowers. Even Abel stopped his crawling.'

'Abel was present when, when….'

Once again I choked on my words.

This woman in front of me had the moral scruples of a dirty dish cloth. But she heard me not.

'"Baudelaire! The pleasures of the nights is comparable with a glass of Constantia wine. Oh how I love Baudelaire. When I am grown up I will go and live in Europe. I fell in love with the Continent last year. I have not told Father yet, for I am to take his place and farm sunflowers or become prime minister of this land, oh the idealistic dreams of parents seeped with toxins for a young soul filled with aspirations of travel on the dusty roads of Spain following in the footsteps of peasant poets and story tellers, for I am Pascual Duarte, my life brimming with pain and bad luck, how will I break the news to my father? Will you? Oh please say you will,

woman as pretty as the sunflowers, my father will
doubtless lend his ear to your words of wisdom. For I
want to dine with Cela and Galdoz, drink red wine and
not worry about this," he shouted with his hand on his
hips. What choice did I have Kaner my Son, life took all
my choices away when an unknown woman placed me
on a the steps of a church.'

'Mother, that is a pathetic excuse for becoming a
whore?'

I bit my tongue. It was too late. The words hung
between us. She stared wide eyed at me.

'Leave now you spawn of the devil,' she said the words
softly, 'there is no place for you in this house.'

Slowly our conversations of old returned. I noticed
she casted her eyes all too frequent down and withdrew
into silences from where she did not return for some
time. I tried my best not to stare.

Tiny fat hands preyed us apart. Her pleading voice
caught me off guard.

The three of us spent the afternoon catching-up on a
blanket on the weeds under the fig tree, we had so much
to talk about, questions to ask, stories to tell, she asked
several times after the General, what does he look like
now?

'Have you met him?'

'Once, a long time ago.'

I noticed her half attempt at pushing her hair into
some sort of style.

It failed, the dead strands unruly, listlessly resting on
her shoulders.

'When, where?'

'Down there,' she pointed at the other side of the hill.

'In the sunflower fields?'

'Mmm.' She looked at her fingers, not into my eyes.

'What happened Mother Abishag, how long ago?'

'Long ago, too long.'

She drifted off into a reverie and I was unable to coax her back to the present.

She placed her head on my lap, I stroke the brittle hair. Oh Mother Abishag, what had happened to you?

Mother Abishag drifted off into a restless sleep prattling nonsensical words. Mara seemed the only one who understood as she chattered back in her baby language.

I rested my head against the fig tree bark.

Blue skies above, did the Ibis ever found his tribe after being swept away in the sandstorm? Or does he sit on the side of the chariot near Father?

Dina cooked dinner, we ate outside at a table under the tree. The candle flames suspended still in the night air. The frogs still croaking reassuringly from somewhere below in the sunflower fields. Mother Abishag disappeared inside carrying a sleeping Mara against her chest. Dina sat down next to me, bent over in a confidential manner.

'Your Mother Abishag is not well, not well at all.'

'What do you mean Dina?'

'Her sugar, she has blood sugar problems. Diabetics, the doctor said, she takes medication, injections.'

'When did this happen, who injects her?'

'A few months after the birth, it's serious Kaner Boy, lock your bedroom door tonight, your shock arrival will do her no good, she injects herself, when she remembers, sometimes she forgets she is ill, then she kind of gets funny, wild. I inject her, when the attack is mild, many times I call Johannes from next door, I now have a phone in my room, sometimes, well......'

Her voice drifted off.

'Well, what, what happens.'

'I can do nothing, I watched from behind my window, protecting my daughter and I from the mad woman running naked in the garden, she talks to herself, I just wait and wait. She falls asleep, I drag her back into bed, the next morning she wakes up, remembering nothing.'

'Mara, what happens to Mara?'

'Nothing, she dotes on your sister, it keeps her going, its all she has now. Some night I watched her walking around the garden, she even climbs up into the tree, where she sits, talking to herself. No one comes here anymore. Boss Jacob used to, but he stopped. I think he sends money every month, what she does with it I have no idea, your Mother Abishag pays me to keep my child healthy and dressed. I think you must go to Rest-and-Peace Kaner, claim what is rightfully yours. I was there, remember, my ear pressed against the dining room door when oubaas Jack said you and Abel must get some farmland, I was curious, the white people's business our coloured people's poison chalice.'

I was shocked, half hearing what Dina said, not taking it all in, is that why Mother Abishag looked so run down, unkept, uncared for?

I thought it was because she missed Father. Or had money problems.

I must talk to her about money, how did she survive, family hand outs I guessed. She could not afford a lawyer to contest the wills and whims of the Du Preez's. Where did the General fit in, was he setting us up, having Alex assassinate for his own gain?

Dina nodded and sighed. Mother Abishag appeared in the door, portable record player in hand. She sat back down on the blanket and put a needle on the record. The soothing sounds of Pohjola's daughter floated gently into the night.

I laid back, crossed my arms behind my head, above my head the stories of my childhood played out on the stage of the night.

I stole side glances at Mother Abishag, so different, but still Mother Abishag, so normal looking. Like a desert flower, desperate for rain, but sustaining itself. I noticed her attempt at dressing up, a dead rose tugged behind her ear.

Our bedroom sat unchanged.

I rummaged through the drawers, I sniffed Abel's clothes until I found an unwashed piece of clothing faintly stained with his distinct body smell, I took it to bed with me. Familiar night shadows danced on the ceiling.

I looked at the floor, the night mice no longer a threat. I missed Abel, the bed opposite empty. He strong body not there. I slipped my hand under the sheet. My brother filled my mind as I stained the sheets.

The bedroom door flung open. A dark shadow spilled into the room. Reaching out for me long before the upright body moved forward. Mother Abishag!

A mad woman. Not my Mother Abishag. Mara clutched under her arm like a loaf of bread. She walked towards me, pointing a dirty fingernail in my direction. Her face awry.

'Your dirty little fuck, how dare you come back into my house, you who stole my babies, you dirty whore, you think I did not know what you were up to all those years. I want you out. Go!'

Mara started to cry.

'Look! She fears you, I fear you, you evil child with the scarlet red hands, not even the spiders will touch you, your evil eyes cursed this house. The deviance of God is wrapped in you, why did you come back, why?'

She moved closer to the bed.

I jumped out, holding my hands up in self defence.

'Mother Abishag, please, its me, Kaner, your son, what are you saying?'

Did my words sink in.

She placed Mara on the bed. I steadied my shaky legs against the bed. What was I suppose to do, hit her, wrangle this mad woman to the floor. Kill her to save us all?

'Don't you look at her with your evil eyes, avert, avert your eyes now! You filthy bastard child, I hated you from the time you arrived in my womb. You devoured me from the inside, how I loathed each moment with you inside my womb. I tried, god knows I tried to rid myself of you, tenacious as a desert weed you were, making me wretched, you despicable piece of villainous vermin. I never thought you would survive the desert, I instructed him to kill you off, erase the stain from my name. Why are you back in my life, to take my child from me?'

I clasped my hands in prayer position, silently pleading with her in desperation to end this madness as rage and hatred and confusion competed in me.

How could I hit my mother, this was not my Mother

Abishag.

With one arm she reached for my neck. I reached for the backpack.

Her puffy eyes followed my every movement, cautiously, guarded.

I pulled a blue vial and silver syringe out. Dina's baby blue eyes on me too.

My eyes flicked to the window. Outside the night was dark, no moon tonight, no fairytales, where was the owl, hunting down the scurrying creatures of the night?

'Kaner no!'

Dina screamed from the door. The baby cried.

Confusion.

Anger.

What is it with women.

'She does not know what she is doing, this is not your mother, this is a human being craving sugar. Help me put her on the bed.'

Mother Abishag starred bewilderedly from Dina to me, her madness wavering. She fought us like a possessed vixen as I wrestled Dina from her arms.

The baby cried.

Mother Abishag spat into my face as I forced her to the floor with brute force.

Dina pushed the needle in. Mother Abishag slumped into a deep coma.

We laid her to rest in Abel's bed. The kookiness gone, her mouth twitching, was the demonic conversation continuing in her mind?

'This is wrong Dina.' I cradled Mara in my arms.

'Its nature, she can't help it, tomorrow all will be forgotten, do not remind her of tonight, promise me K, she will not understand, the words she spoke are not hers, She accused me of far worse, your mother loves you, she always did.'

'But why did she said what she said? How can I not believe?'

'You have to son, you are a grown-up man, I could not believe my eyes when I saw you today, how proud your Father would have been proud of you, the little barefoot boy turned into a beautiful young man, your hair and beard, oh how I wish my mother could see you, you were her favourite, she always wondered what went on in your head when your eyes focused on nothing, one day he will achieved big things, Mother Abishag had instincts about you. Mother Abishag, Fay died six months ago, in her sleep, did you know?'

Dina turned around, not waiting for an answer, covering her eyes like a desert walker against the morning sun and walked out of the room, the faint cries of her baby somewhere in the night.

I took the syringe, filled it from the blue vial and shared the contents between the three of us, we all deserved engineered dreams, even Mara.

I climbed in the bed, pulled Mother Abishag's head on my lap, held Mara in my arms and kept my finger on her tiny heart, monitoring the slowing, she closed her eyes as she drifted off into sweet and innocent infant dreams.

If only I could open my mind cage and let the Hadida fly off into her imagination, providing her with escape from this nocturnal real nightmare she innocently watched when alone with our raving mad mother. Mother Abishag returned to normal.

Her blue pools of purity opened with sunrise.

I said nothing.

Her words churned inside me like a maelstrom, which one of the two brothers caught in the classical tale was I, will I be driven mad in time by the horror spectacle I witnessed, or will the beauty of her words be revealed with time, making me stronger to survive?

Who I am really, what are people's feelings towards me, who can I believe, if deep within the recesses of my mother's mind pure evil existed towards me?

I left two days later without explanation.

I washed and coloured her hair.

I clipped her nails. I stocked the cupboards with food. I bought Mara and the coloured child of Dina clothes. A quiet child, a snot eating child, watching the world go by with puppy eyes.

Dina I left Camp Basawa currency. I said I will leave word with Abel to visit.

I made no promise of a return visit. I left paper on the kitchen table. One stack blank and empty, the second stack filled with Zulu scribbles, page after page after page. I will post a dictionary.

I said nothing, just left it there for her to discover in her own time.

I watched her through the opening of the bedroom door sitting at the dressing table chair, a shaky hand pushing the needle into the thigh.

She looked old, tired of life, ridden with a burden she carried alone. What was to become of her, I was not sure, for now, I pushed her to the back of my mind, I needed Abel by my side, his advice and guidance to make sense of it all.

I took the bus to Beaufort-West.

My head rested against the window, not blacked out this time, watching the arid landscape passing by, leaving the two greying, ageing bitches and their puppies, free from tethers, behind in their kennel.

## *Inside the City of Gold!*

Tracking Julius was easier than anticipated. I was in a rush. I would rather the mission destination was somewhere through dense jungle vegetation than the City of Gold concrete jungle with its thousands of humans milling around me.

The ants spilling from their nest, people flowing constantly onto streets, going somewhere, and the first few hours I found myself standing on street corners, watching them going about their ways, milling from their food stockpile and sleep repositories to tall concrete mounds where they sat next to each other for hours doing seemingly aimless tasks.

They were a different breed of human from the ones I had encountered in my life so far. They were almost always not smiling, hard faces with a destination only the magnetised pointers in their heads were programmed to know, always in a rush, the city people.

Were they in a hurry to come back, were they ever nervous not finding their way back home, I just did not know.

Unlike ants spilling from a nest with the common purpose of finding food, stopping along the way, using sounds and touch as communication tools indicating the route, the city people mostly ignored each other, on the odd occasion someone did stop to talk to a stranger, the stopped stranger was almost always in a hurry to proceed, with a grimace of annoyance, as if in pain, directions shown reluctantly or shoulders shrugged in ignorance.

A strange world to the uninitiated.

It was my first time in a big City. Module City Life was not a feature in the Camp Basawa syllabus. Was there a need?

I assumed they assumed humans interact universally irrespective of the number of concrete mound holes surrounding the movement of humans.

Open hand combat must be equally effective in fighting enemies crawling from behind dense vegetation and enemies lurking around artificial concrete mounds.

I was given a phone number. I called the number from a phone outside City of Gold Central Station soon after I stepped off the overnight train, forty eight hours from the time I left the house on the hill behind.

One train a day passed through Beaufort West where I made my connection from Peaceful Glen.

I had slept little on the train, my mind was with Mother Abishag and Penny-Pitstop and the life they led.

Fortunately the train was quiet. Nearer to the front of

the steel caterpillar sprinting across the sunburned and moonlit landscapes the second and third class accommodation were crowded.

I sat by myself in the first class compartment.

I left the starched sheets untouched. At the dirty streaked window I sat, watching the country sped by as I headed north into unknown territory.

The open spaces were sporadically interrupted by sleeping villages and nameless towns. Black and brown kids from the lokasies on the outskirts holding out hands for food and money as the train passed them by.

Small round faces with big white eyes and rows of shiny white teeth gazing from the dirt tracks along the railway line.

Secret faces waiting to be stapled to folders. An old lady voice answered the phone.

'I am Karelia.'

'I am Pohjola's daughter,' she replied in a husky voice, 'who send you?'

'My father.'

'How is he.'

'Old, his beard is long and white.'

'What are you wearing?'

'A cloth of gold.'

'Where are you from?'

'The dusky landscapes.'

'Why are you here?'

'To kill the evil spirits with an axe.'

I followed her instructions and arrived at a red brick building next to Joubert Park.

Her name was Vera, she had long grey hair tied into a tight bun at the back of her head and was the oldest person I ever met, older than Grandma Esther. Emerald green eyes were hidden behind a deep wrinkled skin. She spoke the Queen's English, no trace of the harsher local English accent.

The tiny figure stood in the doorway, staring at me, transfixed, was it dampness I detected in her eyes?

The old lady shook her head as if to clear it, and invited me in. She wore a black dress with thick grey socks underneath. On each of her fingers glittered a precious stone set in gold. She held both hands out to my admiring eyes.

'The best safe for a lady's jewels. My lovers and husbands were generous, draping my fingers with the precious stones from the rich African soil, I beguiled them, returning their investments with high interest.'

The one bedroom flat was small. Everywhere carton boxes stood stacked up to the ceilings. Three Siamese cats perched on the living room boxes. Their rich blue almond shaped eyes followed my entrance cautiously.

I touched my own eyes instinctively. We viewed each other with suspicion, I had no doubt they would hurl themselves at me should I dare to harm the hands opening their tinned food every morning.

'Take a seat young man,' Vera said.

She disappeared into the kitchen.

Seating choice was limited, newspapers, magazines and piles of papers were stacked on the two chairs and sofa, the only available space was where she sat, two knitting needles and a half knitted red and black jumper reserving a space for her.

I took a pile of magazines from the sofa and placed it on the floor. The cats kept a watchful eye on me.

I was tempted to make a scary monster face, but my courage wavered at the prospect of three cats catapulting in my direction and lashing out at my face. A portrait of the Queen of England hung on the wall next to a photo of Ian Smith.

Vera shuffled back into the room with a tray. On the tray stood a tea pot under a knitted cosy and a plate filled with finger biscuits covered in sugar.

My stomach rumbled, a reminder of the time that had passed since the early morning breakfast served by the waiter in his starched Jacket as the sun poked its head above the fast moving horizon. She poured us tea and placed the plate with biscuits next to me, squeezed in between the magazines and my thigh.

'My golly, they recruit you boys younger and younger nowadays. In my younger days the men arrived with full grown moustaches and beards, now the Boss sends me munchkins with bum fluff on their chins. How old are you child?'

'Old enough to travel of my own, I am sixteen,' I replied proudly.

'Dear oh dear,' she said with a tit-tit of her tongue, 'I dread to think how concerned your dear mother must be. How is your dear mother?'

I did not reply. This was Mother Abishag's choice for us.

Mother Abishag's face invaded my mind, I shook my head in an attempt to rid my mind of it.

Was it only four nights ago when the fat wild haired woman appeared in my bedroom doorway?

'Do you know my mother, how?' Vera waved her hand dismissively in the air.

'No, no, we all have mothers don't we, and they are all dears, one day when you are my age you will think with fondness of your mother, if you don't do so now.'

'My...my mother,' I clasped my hand over my mouth, stopping the intended words, I could not discuss what I saw and thought of my mother with this stranger, the woman responsible for me sitting on this sofa. I was no longer convinced Mother Abishag only had our best interests at heart. Vera interrupted my thoughts.

'I was once your age you know, my Mother Abishag took decisions I did not understand. She married a foreigner and shipped us out to Rhodesia, denying me and my sisters the right of growing up in our native England. Imagine that. But what could we do? Mother Abishag did what she thought was right.'

'What was it like living in Rhodesia?'

'It was good child, very good, special. But it ended so sadly. I fled in the end, like a frightened dog with my tail between my legs, or should I say with my handbag. Look around you, this is all I have left, my life, my memories in boxes. My dear neighbour braved his life sending what he could. I watched my husband being hacked to death, right there he lay in a puddle of his own blood. I would be next, but the shoulders showed up in time, killing those cold hearted bastards ready to hack a cowering woman when their mothers brought them up to respect a woman. I fled, l had no choice, women do not always have choices child, we just do what we have to do to live our lives.'

Her voice trailed off.

Sad eyes gazed longingly at the photo of Ian Smith. She rummaged through the pile of papers on the coffee table to her side and pulled a brown folder out.

The crinkly old face suddenly became serious. She handed me the folder.

'Julius Nyele, enemy number one, full of bravado, full of words, words of hatred. If he had his way, he would open up the arsenals of the army and give each of his fellow country men a rifle or machine gun to mow down the whites. The Boss told me you are here to eliminate the enemy of the state.'

Her voice was cold, her eyes locked me down. The transformation from old lady to ice maiden was sudden, taking me by surprise, the second sudden change of character in so many days. How different from men they are.

I looked up.

The cats sat upright.

'Beware of him, you are not the first attempting termination. The previous two boys were found hacked to pieces, they were older than you. Julius is clever, fearless, his ambition to lead this country into civil war a fire consuming his soul. Why they do not take him out and make him disappear is beyond me.'

Her eyes darted over me, assessing my capability to take out an enemy of the white state.

'You are different, younger, prettier, I will not ask after your instructions, the Brigadier knows what he is doing, always did. You must be one of his protégés. Karelia, hmm, he still does surprise me.'

Her voice trailed off.

She looked down at her hands, twisting the red ruby ring on her left pinky around and around. One of the Siamese cats jumped down and rubbed itself against the leg of its owner, closing its eyes whilst purring.

Vera picked the cat up and rubbed the soft, glossy fur around the elegant neck.

'Karelia meet Karelia.'

The cat opened its oblique eyes and greeted me in a low-pitched sound. Did it recognized my oblique eyes? I tried opening my eyes wider.

'You called it Karelia,' I asked, surprised at the coincidence. Was the cat working for the Brigadier as well, I could not suppress the snicker welling up inside. 'How unusual, do you know the story of Karelia?'

She ignored my question and comment, volunteering information on her terms.

'Julius arrived back from his village five days ago. You will find him at the fountain in the park late in the afternoons, with his new friend, the Argentinian, my sources are not sure where he came from. They play music. Julius plays the saxophone and the Argentinian a flamenco guitar, they attract a crowd each day I believe, safety I reckon. Julius safeguards himself when in public, maybe the Argentinian is  a body guard. Do you play an instrument?'

'Yes, the flute.'

Her eyes narrowed, she pointed both index fingers at me, the sun bounced off the three diamonds on the left finger and the wedding band on her right finger.

'Be careful, be very careful, keep to yourself until the time is right. It's time for this to end. Another life can not be wasted for nothing. You will not be the first attempting a killing. A young man, older and with a bigger build than you sat in exactly the same spot as you twelve weeks ago, and six weeks before him, and three months before the last one. The police found them in a backstreet of Hillbrow, burned out tires around their necks. The scumbags are one step ahead of us. They have an informant somewhere, but who? You boys are trained in keeping secret. African justice is swift, this is not a game for children, hence me checking your age, well, I must trust his judgment, mustn't I?'

She muttered the last words to herself.

'What is wrong with your hand child, your left fingers seem crooked?'

I looked down at my hand, it was true, my fingers had never been the same since Jaubert crushed them, the index fingers bent outwards in a contorted way. I hid my hands between my legs. 'Nothing, its nothing, just training.'

'You take extra precaution Karelia, keep your facilities alert, trust your instincts, sniff the danger, the threat of those swines and murderers.'

Her eyes drifted down from my face and came to rest on the tattoo on my neck.

She stared intently.

'Why a hammerkop, you love birds?'

I nodded and touched my trophy hammerkop tattoo, in honour of mission accomplished, in honour of the dead Scorpion Soldier.

'It's protection against the curse, the hammerkop wards off evil curses, I have been cursed twice, Kuyu, a tribal boy in the camp drew the tattoo.'

Vera rose from her chair.

Karelia leaped from her lap, and with the other two cats in tow, lead the procession from the living room, down the corridor and to the front door.

Vera handed me a key from the back of the door.

## Fire & Desire

The room was on the seventh floor.

It was small, furnished with a single bed, a fridge, a two plate cooker, a wooden rocking a chair and a turntable, no records, I half expected Sibelius.

Behind a worn red velvet curtain hung jeans, shirts and a few oversized jumpers from pegs on the wall. Plain black and white T-shirts stacked on a shelf.

A shower and toilet hidden behind a plastic curtain. Sparse living conditions but I did not mind.

For the first time I had a room to myself, I did not share, I had no one else to consider, just me.

I eyed the bed, in a hurry for a day dreaming session without the interruption of other boys or even Abel.

I placed the vials in the fridge, 18 days remained, I had 18 days to release the human engineered poisonous fuse of nature's vicious forces into a human blood stream and watched the violent reaction. Once back in the camp, the scientists would expect a debriefing, pounding me with questions, their eyes glazing over as I relayed the reaction, the violent spasms, the skin colour tone changes, the dark blobs appearing under the skin as poison raced down the human blood channels carrying their fatal cargo to the centre of the human life, the heart, slowing down the pulse, like a high-speed train coming to a halt at the dead-end of the track, the spirit of life disembarking and disappearing into the throng of departed spirits. The journey over, lifeless eyes staring up at the blue sky and the scientists taking up their mark at the benches, at the ready to milk another oversized viper and extract the amber-coloured liquid from the repulsively distorted laboratory grown black scorpions.

I showered and climbed naked into the bed and pulled the sheets over my head, I was in need of sleep, my head was filled with Vera's stories and the events of the last few days Peaceful Glen.

The wall clock ticked-ticked hypnotically. I wondered what an Argentinian looks like before sinking into a deep sleep, the files contained no information on him.

There I laid wide eyed for a while. I thought in the back of my mind. Thoughts about people and places.

How I was here.

On a small little bed. In the City of Gold. And not somewhere else.

How suddenly I no longer shared a room with Abel.

I turned my face to the other side of the room. The bed Abel slept on stood not there. Nor the bedside cabinet with my favourite books.

I felt not sure how I felt about the changes in my life.

160

No longer was I a boy who went to school.

Who sat by the athletic field and pool watching other boys fool about in the water. I was a boy who worked. Not even sixteen and involved in state business of enemies and men who kill for a living.

There were so many other interesting things to do in life.

How did I end up here doing this. The decision of our Mother. Her act to sleep with the sun of the farmer caused the circumstances of my crazy life. Circumstances.

Hastily made decisions affecting the lives of others. Now it was my turn. If I kill Julius, I affect his life. Like I affected the live of Bokero.

Would anyone know it was me. Would Julius know the circumstances. Tonight could almost be like two forces colliding under difference circumstances. Slowly I drifted from the waking world to a dream.

In the forest of my dreams distorted representations from the void of my reality haunted the dream I.

A faceless persona I knew was me. I tried to find a mirror, mirrors do not exist in dreams.

The dreamer never sees his own face the dream. An faceless, nameless identity. Yet, I knew it was me.

Mother Abishag sat naked in the garden filled with overgrown shrubs and piglets running around her, a scorpion tale growing from her backside.

She looked up with a face showered with supreme pleasure. A baby boy she held in her arms. She held the baby out to the I in my dreams.

I took a step forward. It was a beautiful baby. The child grimace at me. Held his hands out. I wanted to take him from the arms of Mother Abishag.

The scorpion tale rose up in the air. Midair its shadow fell over the baby. Instinctively I reacted to rescue the little cherub. The scorpion stung me. I felt the onset of the paralysis. I knew I started to die. I looked up at the face of Mother Abishag

'Why,' I asked with bitter tears rolling into my mouth.

I swallowed my unknown sorrow as I watched the thin lips under her substantial nose unbarred into a leer.

'It's my nature,' she replied.

I knew it was over for me when stinger hoisted me into the air and smashed me down. I shouted and woke up in a cold sweat just before it was time for my skull to be crashed.

It was just gone past six o'clock. Despite the dream I felt refreshed.

'Bloody Mother,' I muttered, then jumped from the bed.

I felt hungry. From the fridge I took a bottle of milk, a pack of sliced salami and a banana. I devoured the food. The rumbling in my stomach stopped. In the shower I let the cold water stream over my body.

I thought of masturbating but decided against it, concerned shooting my juice now down the shower drain might affect my evening performance.

The clothes left in the little apartment fitted like a tailor cut it. I wore a pair of jeans and a white T-shirt. A glance in the mirror reassured me I looked dapper to say the least, rather butch. It felt good no wearing the stupid camp clothes. The fit was perfect. Did Vera shop for the clothing? I wore a white T-shirt. It felt good not wearing black combat clothes. I was now one of them, a civilian. I wiggled my toes in the flip flops. I felt confident I would outrun the enemy barefoot.

I leaned out of the window. The pavements and streets filled with people rushing about, people disappeared into the openings of the blocks of flats along the park. The city hummed, a sea monster swallowing the plankton drifting in the current.

Excited I removed the flute from the backpack, I was in hurry to join the bustling life below. I scanned the park from the window, but was unable to locate the fountain. How different this Friday evening was from the ones in the camp. The boys would be down on their arms pushing their body weight up to the count of the sergeants. The late heat of the day hit me in the face, it was different to the bone-dry Camp Basawa desert heat.

No misty moisture creeping over the dunes. The cement heat was oppressive, artificial, trapped alongside the scurrying people between the concrete walls. No escape route, unlike the hot air rising from the desert floor.

I crossed the street. A flame-red haired woman in a faded pink leather skirt stopped me in front of the park gate. She placed a hand, with excessively long finger nails, on my chest. The nails were painted orange-red in a failed attempt to match the colour of her hair.

A cigarette dangled from the other hand in a Humphrey Bogart style attempt, whether consciously or unconsciously I was not sure, but all she achieved was obscuring her destitute eyes in smoke.

'Oh how cute,' a raspy voice jumped from her throat, 'a new kid on the block. I watched the little chicken crossing the road, just in case I should sweep tail feathers from the street. Dora has not seen you here before. Dora offers young boys special discount on a Friday night even if her black book is rather busy, I will make room for you.'

She burst out into raucous laughter.

'Oh well, as you are so young and Dora adores the taste of veal, I may just let you slip it in for free, how about that my little cock-a-doodle-doo?'

The nicotine stained finger trawled the outline of my ears and beard. The crook of her arm punctured with dark purple needle pricks. The hand on my chest dropped and hitched the already tight leather skirt further up, more needle pricks, the woman was a living pin cushion.

'What do you say honey, you look tongue-tied to Dora, has your Mummy never shown you what a real woman's treasure box looks like, jewels honey jewels, I have them all inside here, put your hands inside and glide over Dora's precious possession. The city men kill for the opportunity.' I shook my head, not quite sure what this vision meant or what I was suppose to say. The smell wafting into my nostrils was rather unpleasant, a pungent smell reminiscent of the skeleton coast with its rotten sea life, briny. I saw enough jewels for one day.

'Later, maybe later,' I mumbled and walked away, I was rather unnerved by this woman, not quite sure what to say or do. A letter bomb killer encountered in the jungle I could handle, a walking city jewel box left me hesitant. Inside the safety of the park, I turned around, but Dora was bent over talking to the driver of a car pulled up at the kerb, her fascination with me short-lived.

Inside the park the sea monster humming died down. City dwellers sat around on the lush green grass drinking wine, or sat on benches paging through newspapers and reading books. It was a haven, I felt at ease, relaxed. I scanned the park, through the hedges on the south side the light of water glimmered.

I followed the path, hearing musical notes drifting into the air, a small crowd guarded the  music source. I walked around the edge of the gathering. Two men sat on a rock at the side of the water lily filled pond. In the background the water cascading over the rocks accompanied the live music unobtrusively.

I stood transfixed.

It was them, no mistake. It was Julius and the Argentinian.

My heartbeat increased until I willed it slower. Julius was a fine looking black man, broad shouldered with bulging biceps, flexing with each pressing of the keys, thick lips captured the mouthpiece, eyes closed, the white t-shirt caressing the rounding of his pecs, firm, rounded buttocks encased in jeans stretching as he bent forward beguiled by the dark jazz sounds floating around his head, a barefooted giant he was.

He was a great specimen of a human, he reminded me of a black Abel. My eyes moved left.

My heart missed a beat,  oxygen rushed through my blood.

Long black hair covered the face of the Argentinian bent over the flamenco guitar, the fingers of a passionate lover stroking the strings, the black t-shirt stretched tightly over the thick muscled shoulders and down the thick triangular muscle running down the side of his body, softly rippling with the playing of the guitar.

I willed him to look up, slowly the crown of hair rose

up and our eyes met across the water pond. His eyes dark pools filled with mystery from a world I had never visited. He smiled, passionate lips parting to reveal two rows of white teeth, a dark stubble lined the strong jaw, I was in awe. I felt intoxicated and light-headed and moved away, sitting down on the grass.

The Argentinian eyes followed me.

Our eyes locked before he bent over and his thumb drummed on wood. The African jazz music infused with Spanish sounds was unlike any other music I heard before. I wished Abel and Mother Abishag were with me.

The music stopped. The crowd applauded, the musicians bowed. The crowd dispersed in different directions when the two men placed the instruments on the grass.

The Argentinian whispered into Julius's ear. Both men looked up. The black man waved me over. I stood up and sauntered in their direction.

'Hello, I am Julius.'

The handshake firm, black fingers folded over my white hand. His English without an accent.

I replied, my accent soft, linguistic lessons coming into the play, it was best not to put the enemy on the back foot with a harsh Afrikaans accent. I returned the firm handgrip with equal strength, the two of us testing and assessing each other's physical and emotional power.

'Meet my friend Salvador-Arana, from Argentina.' Another strong handshake gripped my arm, I matched his pressure, our eyes exchanged mutual appreciation, he pulled me closer in a friendly hug and planted a kiss on my cheek.

'You have a beautiful, soft beard mi corazon, ' his

voice whispered in my ear. The b's exploding softly as he spoke, only a feint trace of weak consonant pronunciation in his voice. The soft warmth of his body pressing through my T-shirt. I half expected a false identity, but no, this was passport introductions. Vera's warnings temporarily forgotten in the presence of the two outwardly warmhearted men.

'You have the fingers of a matador,' I replied as I freed myself from his embrace. He brushed his hair back, I copied his movements.

'You play?' Julius said, I nodded.

I placed the flute between my lips and pushed the air for the first notes of Cucurrucucu Paloma through. Salvador-Arano joined in promptly and a few seconds later the three of us were lost in the universal language of music, three men, yes I know I was barely sixteen, but the boy had been put to eternal sleep many moons ago, secluded from the world beyond the fence of the park, the city bustle, the laws of the land, the instructions of our masters, paused on the collision course of our lives. Julius invited me to dinner with the two of them.

I declined, I needed to break the spell, the magical intimacy was overwhelming, I wanted to step away, clear my head, break the spell and regroup.

First contact was established, remain in control, keep the initiative. The subliminal messages of my master's voice powering my actions.

'Can we meet later?' I asked.

'Where do you live?' Julius asked. I hesitated, what if they wanted to come over? 'With my grandmother, across the road.' I pointed to the high rise buildings surrounding the park, nowhere specific.

'We will come and collect you after dinner,'

'No, can I meet with you somewhere?' I was lax, Vera's file open on the bed, photos of the black man standing in front of me scattered on the pillow.

'We are going to the Hanging Tree club in Melville tonight, have you been?'

I shook my head, the road from the station to Joubert Park was all I knew.

A club? What happens at a club? My excitement bubbled over.

I nodded my consent. City life was growing on me. Would I cope?

No Camp Basawa module prepared me for this kind of excitement. 'We can't teach you everything,' Moshe used to say, 'make it up as you go along, let your instincts take over, we train you do your job, when your instincts fails you, the ingrained training takes over, you have been chosen for who you are, what you are capable of on your own, we only enhance the tools of nature.'

Julius scribbled the address on the back of an empty cigarette box and handed it to me. With promises of seeing each other later, we parted ways.

I stole a sneak peak back at the two of them, just to be caught in the act as the two of them already turned back, watching me leave the park.

### What a time to be alive!

I waved and disappeared.  I looked for Dora, she was
nowhere to be seen.  I could have asked her what to wear,
expect from a night at the Hanging Tree. What if she
warned me not to go?

I ran up the stairs to the first floor and knocked on
Vera's door. Her footfall shuffled down the corridor, she
looked pleased to see me.

'I met them,' I gushed.

Vera jerked me into the flat and closed the door
behind her after she glanced up and down the corridor.
'Hush child, the corridors have ears.'

Vera was dressed in her nightgown, a faded red gown
with a peacock embroidered on the back. I followed her
into the kitchen, she opened the fridge and assembled a
ham and cheese sandwich without asking. I was grateful,
the excitement left me starving. City life was hungry

work, was that why the people were always in a rush, hurrying to find food, the worker ant rushing back to eat its own fungus?

Karelia glided into the room and flung herself against my leg. I devoured the sandwich and bag of crisps Vera placed in front of me. She opened a bottle of beer. From the pocket of her gown she removed a small eye drop bottle, she measured ten drops into the beer.

'There Kaner, it's Friday evening, wash your food down.'

In between bits of bread I relayed the afternoon's events to Vera. She listened, nodding every so often, never interrupting the story.

'So what do you think,' I asked, 'shall I meet them, what if.....'

'What if what, child?'

I wished she stopped calling me child.

'Vera, do you mind not calling me child, a child killer I certainly am not.' She chuckled at my feeble humour attempt.

'What if they suspect my intentions?'

'And what are your intentions?'

'Julius is a nice man, I liked him, but I have to take him out, and so is the Argentinian, I found him mesmerising, foreign, exotic, his fingers stroked the guitar passionately like a lover making love with all his heart.'

Vera watched me intently, her wrinkly eyes narrowed slightly. She took my hands in hers and pressed hard.

'Listen Kaner, and listen carefully to me. Life is a war. We are in war with them. The only reason your mother and I can sleep in warm beds under freshly ironed sheets

170

tonight is because we fight them, we keep them in their place. That black man may well come across as nice, but, it is a front, just like you are a nice boy, sorry, young man. Read your file, read the speeches he delivered. He is a man prowling the township underworld at night, inciting hatred for the white skin, he will slit your throat, without hesitation, if he so much as catch a whiff of your intentions, so will the Argentinian, we have no idea who the Argentinian is, he arrived out of the blue, not through the airports, not through customs at the ports, an infiltrator, like you infiltrated the east coast of Africa. Do not look so surprise sonny, you have a file, we all have files. The only reason the State Bureau is not picking him up is because they want to know his intentions. They suspect he is a KGB agent, send to assassinate our political, and possibly military leaders on the highest level. Now you watch your back, the General would not have dispatched you if he did not believe in you. You are not on your own, you are being watched and followed. Experienced and hardened men guard over you. Your innocence and youth are required to get close to very dangerous men, very close, intimately close, for they are on their guard as much as we are. You are programmed, listen to the voice, follow the voice in your head. Karelia kill.'

Vera hissed the last two words with such vehemence that the cats perched on the worktop looked up from their slumber.

I sat back and winked at Karelia, she jumped down from the worktop and onto my lap, her pale blue eyes scrutinised mine. I nuzzled against her soft fur.

A sigh escaped my lips. I thanked Vera for the beer, the fire was gone from her eyes, she suddenly appeared years older, tired.

I followed her down the corridor, kissed her on the forehead, she smelled of talcum powder and aniseed, a smell drifting into our bedrooms as boys when Mother Abishag baked rusks early in the morning.

I pictured Mother Abishag rising at 4 am to knee the dough. My bestest childhood memory serving my idiotic mind very right in that moment of uncertainty. Every image and every boyhood memory flooded back. On the day preceding the baking day, Abel and I scoured the fields for firewood.

To appreciate the specialness of the moment, you must understand Mother Abishag baked bread on the rarest of special occasions. One sensed her baking mood days in advance. It started with her opening the windows and doors of our ramshackle house on top the hill where Abel and I went about our ways like brothers do. As I mentioned, Mother Abishag did little housekeeping. She was too elegant. Our Mother used to tell Abel and I, 'You must understand the domestic goddess role does not make my pulse react. That thrill I only get from buffing the eating utensils and the glassware.'

'Yes Mother Abishag,' we boys replied in unison. I understood the thrill of Mother Abishag to match the thrill of boy meeting boy, like the afternoon I witness Abel and Matt touching each other in the shower.

Days in advance Abel and I went into the heathlands gathering firewood. Against the oven walls laid stacks of rhinoceros bush, sand olive branches and other fynbos.

Early evening on the eve of the big bake Dina lit the fire inside the oven. Soon the fire roared inside. Hot flames casted from itself into the dry clay and soon strong baking aromas from the last batch wafted through the night air.

At the same time Mother Abishag commenced to slow mix the strong white bread flour Dina grounded on the big smooth river stone. The very same stone Father Isaac used to sharpen his pocket knives and the kitchen knives.

With the heating of the oven the strangers phenomena occurred. The termites living under the floorboards of our house started making noise. Quick tik-tik-tik. The moment the termites in the house started this noise, the termites at a distance in the fields and neighbouring termite nests heard the tik-tik-tik and immediately reacted to it.

A strange and frightening experience. A constant signalling by means of sounds. Eerily and all night long the termites bemoaned the lost of their former palace and the life-history of a former glorious Queen.

By the time the birds settled in their nests and the hand of God painted the sky the colour of dusk, the sky filled with virginal termites. Each termite fluttering their four beautiful wings, then take off to mate and become a Queen of a King.

These nights I slept little. I listened to the termite sounds and I listened to Mother Abishag kneeing and kneeing. By the time sun rose, Dina removed the glowing coals from the oven. Mother Abishag pushed her elbow into the oven, testing it for the right temperature.

Not long after our Mother slipped the baking tins into the oven, the fresh smell of baking wafted into our bedroom to wake us up. With eager eyes and watering mouths we took our seats at the kitchen table. Mother Abishag tortured us. She waited an hour of the bread to cool down.

Then she'd cut.

The bread wobbled under the knife.

Thickly she's spread butter over the warm slices. Glistening gold the melted butter shimmied. Below the earth the honeymoon couples started digging the front doors to their new white ant palaces.

Back in the dark corridor, I stood listening to the sounds. Toilets splattered.

Somewhere a drunk woman shouted smuttiness.

A bottle crashed.

It was a crazy place. Once I heard Vera bolted her five locks and chains on the other side of her front door, I moved on.

Once outside in the corridor, I stood listening to Vera bolting the five locks and chains on the inside of the door. How she must miss her farm.

The smiling young farm woman, standing proudly hand in hand with her husband outside their white washed farm house in the photos on her living room wall, driven out by barbarians such as the one I was about to meet, bloodthirsty savages hunger for revenge, ravaged with desires to settle ancient scores of battles lost by their ancestors against our forefathers.

Back in my room I did a hundred push-up and doubled the number for sit-ups, before crouching like a praying mantis for thirty minutes of silent contemplation, clearing my mind of the day's pollution of thoughts.

I decided on a black T-shirt, another perfect fit. I took the eyebrow pencil liner, I noticed it earlier on a shelf, wondering if a woman stayed here before, and drew two tight lines above the lashes of my lower eye lids.

I stood back and admired the effect in the mirror.

My slanted eyes looked mysterious, dangerous, I felt protected from the evil eye, I just wasn't sure whose eyes were the most evil, mine or theirs. I felt very Cleopatra.

Outside the window darkness clouded the city, a thousand lights shining from the rows of concrete boxes. Inside people went about their Friday night routines.

I took a deep gulp of the warm city air.

What was Abel doing, had he departed on his mission, had he contacted cousin Alex? Suddenly I felt trapped, unsure I could do this on my own, what if I failed to be found with a burning tyre around me?

From the fridge I removed a cobalt blue bottle, my fingers lingered over the vials but tonight was too soon. I lacked confidence to take on both men, even in a cunning way.

What was the Argentinian's secret?

How easily would he tell me, he was unlikely to confess freely, or disclose the darkest recesses of his mind under torture pressure.

I turned around and looked back at the bed. Two pillows. 'Pillow talk,' Moshe taught me, 'the finest and most sophisticated weapon in the secret extraction armoury. A module not on the agenda at his guest tenure at Camp Basawa, Moshe taught the fine art, practiced by the Mossad female agents, of extracting information through casual conversations after a night of passion.

In his arms running my fingers through his dense, curly black chest hairs, he taught me so much more than the rest of the school was privileged too.

Moshe lectured me on the ancient art of
assassination, made me feel proud of whom I am, and
made me understood the abhorrence of society for what
we do.

'We assassins practice ancient rituals, eliminating
threats against our peoples, we do not kill for self gain,
our profession dates back nine thousand years, we are
the only ones capable of keeping check on the men in
power, men commanding armies of thousands,
concocting laws controlling millions, generals and
politicians, the man in the street has no say over them,
the secret cross in the ballot box is only that, a secret,
who knows, who counts, who controls the outcome, the
men in power. I have no fear within, have no shame
within, it is what life on this planet teach us, control over
the strong, control over life. We eradicate, because,
under the thin veneer of society lies the raw essence of
life. Do not be fooled by the fine designer clothes, it's
nothing but a smoke screen, take it away and you will be
faced by an animal with intellectual instincts, we
humans are the finest killers ever to roam this planet, we
are canny, smart and perspicacious.'

I was in awe of this suntanned Israeli, speaking of life
in a way I never thought of, my head resting on his chest
for hours as he talked and talked.

A soft knock on the door spun me around.

I listened.

I grabbed a syringe from the fridge and approached
the door.

'Who is there?'

'The daughter of Pohjola.'

Vera changed into a long white gown, her brushed

grey hair released and falling soft down to her waist. The three cats lined her sides, all three looking expectantly at me.

I pushed the syringe into the back pocket of the jeans. Vera stepped inside.

From her gown pocket she offered me a small Beretta. The killer weapon looked wrong in her wrinkled hands, did she ever kill? Imagining a scene with Vera pointing the weapon at someone's heart was hard, but I was sure she would without flinching.

'You need protection.'

I raised my empty palms to her face.

'Thank you, my hands are all I need.'

Her eyes roamed the room and came to rest on the cobalt blue bottle on the table. She walked over to the table and picked the bottle up.

'Is my son still feeding you lot this?'

She stopped mid-sentence. We both looked at each other. Karelia jumped onto my bed and started pawing the pillow.

'What.....what do you mean, your son?'

Vera abruptly walked out of the room with the bottle in her hand. The cats followed with quick steps, leaving me dumbfounded behind.

I downed half a bottle, I had a sneaky suspicion Vera may just be doing the same, perhaps sharing it with her cats, I sniggered at the thought of Karelia being intoxicated by Camp Basawa nectar, maybe Vera will use her eyeliner on the cats too.

Dora was back on the corner.

'Oh Sweetie, even hotter than this afternoon, you are made for the night, feeling in the mood for Mummy tonight, a goodnight kiss for Dora perhaps?'

She puckered dark red lips at me. I leaned forward and kissed her. She squealed with delight. 'No honey, that one you can have for free.'

I laughed and walked way, up the road, following the directions Julius had given me. The cigarette box replaced the syringe.

The streets buzzed with nightlife, so different and so similar from the desert nightlife, little things crawling around, appearing from nowhere and apparently going nowhere, but each one with its own agenda, programmed to wander with aim.

A few dim stars shone in the night sky.

The silent humming had changed from the afternoon, a deeper guttural growl from deep within the City's lair, luring humans into the night for a taste of undiscovered pleasures.

## *Hanging from the tree !*

The Hanging Tree was located in a quiet tree-lined street.

The soft yellow street lamps transformed the surroundings into a magical fairy garden. The concrete jungle turned soft.

Mysterious.

Excitable.

No longer a little threatened orphan girl standing in the corner of the schoolyard with a looking lost face watching a world, ignorant of her grey washed out hungry appearance, thumbing by.

Now Friday night rolled around. Like magic the girl transformed into a deliciously alluring high-school soda pop fountain at the ready to offer her fruit slams to the creatures of the night, now all dressed up to the nines and ready to bounce.

Walking through the City of Gold streets I gawped at
the beautiful people in their rich and colourful clothes,
like glittering fruits that fell from the sky, they dressed to
a fruity finish.

A tall lanky fellowed dressed like a giant banana. He
walked on the wrong side of the road in the opposite
direction I headed.

He looked like he knew a secret. I took my time
watching him.

'Hey Mister Banana,' I whispered across the city
street, 'where are you going?'

To my surprise he stopped and looked at me. His face
pulled serious like a sheriff who had been asking a
damned good question.

I waited patiently for him to make up his mind. With
a casual wave of his hand, he said, 'I am going as fast as I
can to a a fruity carnival, I don't think I have time to
answer your question.'

'What a funny little banana you are,' I said.

We laughed about it awhile. Then suddenly a dismal
look crossed his banana face.

'What am I doing here,' the Banana dressed man
said, or was he a real banana.

The situation was all too weird. Right there and then,
over the spot where the banana stood it began to rain in
torrents.

The Banana had no shelter. No bucket to pull over its
head.

'Run Banana, run,' I whispered.

It started to run for about a quarter of a mile, crying
and swearing as it did so.

Then it turned a corner and disappeared into the

urban wilderness. With a shake of my head I moved on and turned right at the corner with the abandoned filling station. Instead of fuel pumps, miniature wind pumps slowly whirred.

The blades indicated the direction of the Hanging Tree club. A couple of old men sat on a bench outside the neon sign of an upside down palm tree.

A quick glance in my direction before bowing their heads low in intimate conversation. A black woman with a purple turban at the entrance. Her long red nails stroked her eyebrows.

'Good evening. Name?'

Her voice husky and loud.

'Kaner,' I replied in what I hoped sounded like the big man, Marlon.

The woman consulted a piece of paper on a clipboard, her finger trailing the list of names. One eye brow raised as the finger stopped on Julius. The fine scribble in the comments column undecipherable.

'Welcome to the Hanging Tree Club honey, my name is Gloria, its time to leave your weekday worries on the hanging tree, are you sure you are old enough to handle the honeydew from Gloria's tree?'

'Oh yes, I have never been to a club before, this is my first time.' She smelled rather fabulously and I took a few deep gulps.

'How delightful, a virginal experience, well, now let Gloria tell you something my little black bearded Kublai Khan, tonight, under the roof of this pleasure-dome you will hear and see things opening your eyes, just relax, let the honey-dewdrops Gloria serves guide you through Xanadu for tonight a supernova will explode on stage.'

Gloria took my white hands between her black hands, second time in a matter of hours coloured hands held my hands, her hands soft and smooth, not chapped like Dora's.

'You have the eyes of a poet, you are a traveller, this land is not yours, listen to the maid singing of foreign lands tonight, her words will open your mind so you can make sense of the false Paradise they taught you at school and realise your destiny is not what they want you to be.'

The black woman made no sense, but her words washed into my head, easing the earlier hissing of Vera in my head.

Her voice warm, sultry like the desert night. I liked her, I adored the flattery.

There and then I decided compliments are my new chocolate as I felt rather absolutely fantastic. I decided to sharp up for the big night.

'Follow me, I will place you between the finest warriors of the night, for no other seat in the House of Gloria will do you justice my Ghazi warrior.'

A long shimmering red dress covered her sumptuous curves as she sashayed along the plush red carpet and disappeared through a velvet curtain.

I followed and we walked into a dark smokey room filled with anticipation of the evening performance.

'What do you think my little suave one,' Gloria asked, not looking at me, but keeping her eye on the piano player laughing with a man the size of an opera singer.

'Just right,' I replied, changing my voice intonation from Marlon Brando to one of the 007's, 'this feels like an opera star's powder room.'

'Funny man,' she said, then moved on. Halfway into the room she stopped, turned around and pressed the red finger nail hurting sharply into my chest. Suddenly Gloria yawned.

Quickly I put my hand over her mouth.

'Are you not excited about tonight,' I asked rather anxiously, 'if for nothing else, but my glorious party animal presence.'

Oh boy, how quickly I adapted to the City of Gold night life. I who had not even read the brochure. Look at me now.

'I am so excited,' I said, 'just don't leave me too much to my own devices tonight.'

'No razzias in the House of the Hanging Tree, for Gloria will extract the entrails of the ones ravaging her house personally, understood.'

She turned away wearily.

I nodded, in awe and unnerved, city women were so different from Mother Abishag and Grandma Esther and Dina.

I looked at the ceiling, dear God, what have you brought over me. The euphoric blue vial effect wavering up my legs.

'I will take you with me to Finland one day to warm me in the wintry blisters and stop the preying of the hungry bear,' I whispered into her neck.

She half-turned back, glanced at me from the corner of her eye, smiled, then planted a kiss on my lips.

My first woman kiss.

Oh boy, tonight was the night things were going to happen to me. The taste of her lips I could not place. But what a funny little girl she was.

I wanted to tell her more things, how much I looked forward to the evening, but the majestic black woman moved on.

Perhaps later, around the midnight hour, she and I could go and sit on the roof with a brandy, look deep into each other's eyes and take it from there.

The inside of the club was dark, it was small. I scanned the room.

A handful of tables, red table cloths, lamps with red shades and golden tassels filled the space. The tables were placed in front of a small stage, on the stage stood a stool, a microphone Lola-Lola would have hugged in her day, a pitch black piano to the left and a set of drums and bass violin to the right.

At the rear of the stage a giant, illuminated blue rose draped the back of the stage.

I stared with fascination as the blue veil force swept through my veins, the network of my mind connecting to this dark, underground world in the bowels of the sleeping giant city.

I felt at home, so at home, the thought struck me like lightning, I had found my spiritual home, how many times did Grandma Esther not say the force of light collided in your mind the moment you set foot, for the first time, on the soil of your spiritual home.

This was it!

A bar lined the rear of the club, patrons whispered intimately, raising crystal glasses not out of place on the Rest-and-Peace dining room table filled with rainbow coloured liquids.

The room hummed with low voiced conversation. Fragrant perfume clouded the air. White, coloured and black people mingled with ease as if the laws of the pavement did not apply in here, to them, citizens of a world where apartheid laws were shrugged off from their jewel encrusted shoulders.

I was ready to lose myself in the night, I wished the warthogs were with me, dressed in dinner Jackets and bow ties.

Gloria ushered me to a table in a dark alcove. Julius and Salvador-Arano stood up as we approached the table.

Both men looked dashing in their tuxedos. I glanced around the room, everyone was dressed in evening wear, oh no, I felt a real desert boo-boo, my roots still firmly planted in Peaceful Glen.

'Gloria, bring our friend a Jacket, please.'

Julius said. Gloria ran a hand over my shoulders and arms before walking off.

Salvador-Arano offered champagne, I hesitated, concerned over the clash with the vial contents, the General warned not to drink and drug, the oldest trick of the enemy.

I quickly discarded the warnings, tonight was special, the headiness of my virginal clubbing experience intermixed with the layers of Camp Basawa brainwashing.

The two men offered the chair between them. I sat down, pinched my leg under the table, twice, three times, harder each time.

Am I a grown up now, is this the adult world Grandma Esther always referred to, when she instructed us children should be seen and not be heard?

My name on a list at the door, a table at a club in City

of Gold, how far and foreign today now felt from
yesterday.

I banished a flash of Mother Abishag standing naked
in my bedroom door, not now.

Strangely I was glad Abel was not here, no rivalry for
the attention of the two men, the people in the room, no
overshadowing by my more attractive sibling. Did I look
handsome, did I match my companions?

Conversation was light.

Gloria returned with a purple velvet Jacket. The fabric
felt luxurious on my skin.

Salvador-Arano removed a white carnation from the
flower pot and pushed it into the button hole on my
lapel. He placed his bronze hand over mine folded
around the stem of the champagne glass. How smooth
his hand was, not a trace of a hair on the back.

We raised our glasses, a thousand tiny bubbles
exploded in my mouth, but evaporated before I could
swallow the champagne.

I felt an openness, I could let myself go in the smokey,
darkened cavern below street level, a feeling I hadn't felt
in a long time. Here nothing mattered, amongst these
creatures of the nights,  this mixed bag of colours, who
was the enemy of whom?

I glanced around the room, our table was the only
one filled with all male company. Couples engaged in
intimate conversations, at the bar men and women
whispered and laughed.

Salvador-Arano entertained us with tales of the
fisherman village from Caleta Cordova where he grew
up.

His lisp seductive on my ear as he told us of the long

beach walks where beautiful horses run wild with the wind breezing through their manes. Was he as excited at I at being in a foreign land?

'You come with me one day Amor, you people have no land of your own, I will take you with me.'

The Argentinian leaned back in his chair with a look of pleasant surprise as I replied, 'Si, con mucho gusto.'

Even I was surprised by the force of my memory remembering phrases learned in the heat of the day under the furnace of a canvas tent.

A waitress placed a silver platter laden with opened shells and slimy creatures resting in what smelled like sea water. Salvador-Arano, noticing my hesitation, took a shell and raised it to my mouth.

'Open.'

He cupped my chin in his hand and tilted my head backwards. He deposited the cold morsel. 'Hold it, savour the flavours from the depth of deep oceans, the freedom nature offers to her tiniest creatures, the seductive oysters.'

I sneezed.

'Tabasco,' Julius laughed.

The lights dimmed, conversations died down.

Gloria weaved her way through the tables to the front of the room.

At first I did not recognise her. A larger than life Afro wig adorned her head.

The red dress had been exchanged for a skin tight shimmering golden mini-dress, diamond clusters draped from her ears. Two men walked onto the stage and took position behind the instruments.

'The house is now closed,' Julius whispered into my

ear, ' no taking flight until the lady of house judges the party to be over. Be prepared to hang from the tree.'

A chill ran down my spine as his words took on a sinister meaning.

I eyed the knifes on the table, calculating easy accessed weapons. What did he and Salvador-Arano carry under their Jackets.

'Ladies and my elegant gentlemen I welcome you to the Hanging Trees. This night is special, united we stand in our struggle against white supremacy.

We, the children of Africa, born into slavery on the fields drenched in the blood of our brave warriors from the past. Their souls restless until we set them free with the spilled blood of our oppressors.'

The spot light shone on our table. Julius rose up, turned around and bowed his head to the room.

'I salute our brave leader, a man with a destiny to free us, not to be locked up on an island like the greatest leader of our time. We must protect our fighters, the men tasked with unclasping the shackles of the most evil regime since Hitler roamed up and down the highways of white Europe. A system so evil, event the old reptiles along the Limpopo river have tears streaming down their snouts.'

Salvador-Arano stared intently at me before taking a sip of champagne, wetting his lips only. I glanced at Julius, his face stern, absentminded, his jaw muscle twitched continually.

'Tonight the Hanging Tree is proud to present a very special artist, prohibited from returning to her country of birth, passport confiscated, the world united behind her, honoured her, made her a citizen of the world, smuggled back under the darkness of the night, protected by our handsome friend from the small island off the coast of America. Ladies and gentleman I give you the first lady of our continent. Mother Abishag Africa.'

Silence hushed the dimmed room. The blue rose shone alone.

A petite female figure, shrouded in a purple cape, walked on.

She stopped.

Her eyes scanned the audience. She bowed low and graceful to the audience. Julius stood up, raised a fist in the air and growled, 'Bayete Free Africa!'

The room followed his example, on their feet, fists raised in the air. A united Bayete cry expelled from the audience. Julius walked over to the stage, collecting the red roses from the tables on his way.

With openly expressed admiration he handed the roses to the singer. She kissed Julius on both cheeks. A few words were exchanged.

A waitress placed an ice box with an opened bottle of champagne on our table alongside a bowl with ruby red strawberries and diamond shaped chocolates.

The pianist assisted the singer onto the stool, with an elegant arm sweep she loosened the cape, it dropped to the floor, revealing a much older lady, her waspish hair scraped into a tight bun.

She opened her mouth, a raspy voice, filled with trembling emotions, flowed out. I sat transfixed, all sense of reality evaporated. I hung upside down from the tree of life.

'A long time ago I was a young maiden. Filled with

hopes and dreams of living my life with the man of my dreams. We found each other, happy we walked the under the stars. One day he disappeared. The yellow vans picked him up. He did not carry his pass.'

To my surprise the singer spat on the stage. Memories distorted her face.

'I never saw him again, he vanished from the white concrete bunkers. His bones were left to the vultures on a compost heap. I never stood in front of the altar. I never said I love you, again. My veil was never raised by the man. My bed empty forever. Night after night I waited at the kitchen table, for a knock, a sign, a telegram, a body, but nothing ever showed up. My longing remained unanswered. My questions discarded. Tonight I will share with you my longing for him and for you and this great continent. Songs I sing to audiences around the world, spreading the message of our people captured in slavery like the Israelites of old. I am banished from the deep, dark bloodstained soil of this country I love. One day I will return when our heroes liberated the land of our fathers, when humanity returns and we all can be free like the gazelles of the Kruger Park. When the morning sun returns yellow filled with freedom promises, the shackles removed.'

Her gaze fixed on Julius. Empty butterfly eye sockets floated into my vision. I rubbed my eyes. The singer bowed her head.

The piano hammer hit the strings, haunting notes vibrated into the air. Black tears flowed from the sockets. Salvador-Arano touched my arm.

Reality returned. I downed the glass of champagne, tonight I felt reckless. The bass violin joined in. She opened her mouth. A skylark flew from her mouth and fluttered around the room.

'Igqira lendlela
nguqo ngqothwane,
SebeqAbele gqi thapha
bathi nguqo ngqothwane'

Time stood still, suspended itself whilst the skylark enthralled the audience. Flying high and low with fluttering wings.

She melted into my soul, her voice transported the audience across the dark continent, telling stories of slaves, of wailing mothers, of lost lovers, of the other side, the dark skinned side of the life I never experienced.

I saw Dina stood in the doorway of her bedroom gazing at the night, longing for her mother Fay, sitting outside her whitewashed farmer worker house, bemoaning her lot in private, scrubbing floors, washing clothes, cleaning and clearing up after the white people, how history repeats itself, slavery still not abolished, but enshrined in the law of the land.

Halfway through the concert, Mother Abishag Africa invited Julius and Salvador-Arano onto the stage.

The saxophone and Spanish guitar were brought out by stage hands. The five musicians united as one, upping the tempo and changing the mood.

Mother Africa invited the audience onto the dance floor.

I danced with Gloria, in the back of my mind an infuriated voice riled me, what about the General, Grandmother Esther, I could not imagine she would approve of her grandson dancing with the farm help. Couples gyrated and swung to the beat.

I had fun. Gloria an accomplished dancer, African rhythm pulsated through her veins.

The music stopped, the dancers applauded. Salvador-Arano whispered into Mother Abishag Africa's ear.

She nodded, he returned the guitar to the stand, but Mother Abishag Africa stopped him, she held her hand out, Salvador-Arano handed her the guitar, the little sky lark walked to the edge of the stage, she sat down, looked up at Salvador-Arano and smiled, her fingers stroked the strings, hauntingly beautiful the opening cords of Cuccurucucu Paloma flurried from deep within the hollow cypress soundboard onto the dance floor.

Salvador-Arano jumped from the stage with the grace of a matador, the drummer tapped the first rhythmic beats of the song of lovers and far away countries.

'Dance with me, mia carro.'

He took my hand in his, swung me around, pressed his legs deep between mine and stretched our arms, his breath blowing warm in my neck.

'They say that at nights, all he could was cry all the time.'

Salvador-Arano pushed us across the dance floor, our embrace intimate, our movement exact and passionate.

'He suffered so much for her, that even on his death he was calling her.'

Two stealthy tom cats, pelvises pressed intimately together, the Argentinian moved, I counteracted with equal precision, the captivating bass guitar beat lead by the lonely saxophone and guitar, the emotion filled voice upping the intensity of the dance floor duel.

'That sad sparrow early in the morning goes to sing at the lonely house.'

I closed my eyes, pulled my upper body away, pent-up emotions flowed from my soul into his as wave after wave of sensuality washed over me, I soared into the sky on the back of the Hadida, far below me the river, filled with blood red water, washed everything in its way, away, our little house on the hill, Mother Abishag straddling the roof, screaming at me, holding Penny-Pitstop out, I saw her lips move, her words and the susurrus of the stream did not reach me, up here in the blue sky a silence reigns, all I heard was the flapping of wings as the voice of Salvador-Arano whispered in my ear.

'They swear that that sparrow is nothing else than his soul still waiting for her return.'

Two hearts beating to one sound. The touch of his skin ignited pent-up lava inside me.

I pressed my body closer to his. Our hearts beat in rhythm to the music.

> 'ay, ay, ay, ay, ay, he cried
> ay, ay ay ay ay, he sobbed
> ay ay ay ay ay he sang
> from a deadly passion, he died'
> The wings of the sky lark
> fluttered into the air,
> wing shadows thrown onto the blue rose,
> her eyes closed,
> her spirit carried away,
> her lips moving,
> her longing for what
> no longer was,
> delivered in flight.
> 'Cucurrucucu, cucurrucucu
> cucurrucucu, sparrow don´t cry.'

The music stopped.

Salvador-Arano and I stood still, we did not part, basking in the moment, a single applause broke the spell.

The stage was empty, the skylark vanished underneath the blue rose, her Zulu warrior guarding her back. The floor was empty, the eyes of the room focused on us. Heads bowed down.

Gloria walked over to the decks, placed the headphones on her head, the Afro replaced by long straight black hair.

Hypnotic bass and electronic sounds flooded the club, Salvador-Arano and I swayed to the pulsating throb of the night. I never saw the skylark again, many years flowed by, much blood spilled before I stood before the open grave, a twisted, depleted soul whispering au revoir, at least for now to a departed soul. She died in the only place she loved, the stage.

The sun broke the night panes by the time we bade Gloria goodbye. Salvador-Arano and I sauntered through the deserted streets, bag men and ladies lost in their homeless dreams, wry smiles curved around their mouths.

We drank black coffee at a corner cafe.

He told me about Mother Abishag Africa.

Julius escorted her back to a secret hiding place through the back door of the Hanging Tree.

Life in prison a sure fate if the police caught her without pass and passport.

Julius invited us to the township, he was due to address a political meeting in Soweto later on the Saturday evening.

It took willpower to say goodbye to Salvador-Arana,

breaking the spell, the bond with a man I had just met.

My place or yours not proposed by either of us, we had our own secrets to guard, the time was not ripe to pluck the forbidden fruit, nor were we ready to cross the threshold of our desires, his brief mention of 'my wife awaits my return' stopping any impulsive moves I may have intended.

The words he whispered on the dance floor, without looking at me, were still reverberating in my ear.

'Can I trust you?'

A blinding reality penetrated my mind. 'Kill Karelia kill, but not the Argentine, we do not know who he is, where he comes from, what his mission is.'

I agreed to meet at six for the drive into the townships. I was about to enter the world of the oppressed, the second, nay, third class, if not, classless society.

Back in the flat I tossed and turned, sleep staying away as I battled with the burning desires of my loins. Repressed memories flooded back.

Twenty four hour newsreels replayed on the screens of my mind, occasional pauses, rewinding to understand the magnificence and beauty of the night.

The Argentinian's fragrance lingered in the cavities of my mind, causing conflict and havoc with the feelings I felt for Abel, feelings I had come to terms with over the years. This was different, new, exciting and dangerous.

Did I trust him?

Who could I trust, as rumours of deception of the past washed into my life.

Was the General my father, who was Vera, my grandmother?

Why did Abel say what he said, sowing seeds of distrust in my mind, did he have an agenda of his own, manipulating me to advance his cause?

Finally sleep swept me away into cobalt blue champagne oblivion, Mother Abishag on my dream horizon. My dreams were restless, I stepped off the train onto the lonely platform of Peaceful Glen.

'Welcome to Peaceful Glen' the station board read, 'the penultimate stop on this track, alight now or stay onboard until the end.'

### *Captain Oops!*

The Saturday morning knock on the door was firmer than Vera's the night before.

I listened. The person knocked against the top left panel.

Whoever it was, was tall, left handed. Not Vera, no-one else knew where I lived, was I followed, did Salvador-Arano tail me?

The person knocked again. I waited for their departure. The bedside clock ticked noisily. I was tense, hungover clouds drifting menacingly against the ceiling.

The sun shone bright into the room. I must ask Vera for black out curtains. The knock again, ten times, three seconds between each knock.

I slipped the files under the bed. I opened the fridge door.

Why this blind panic?

Silence.

I watched the clock. It was ten past two, Saturday afternoon in City of Gold. I tip-toed to the sink. My hand hovered above the tap.

Knock-knock-knock.....fifteen knocks this time, each one more urgent, more persistent.

'Fuck this.'

I pushed my head under the cold water. With the towel wrapped around my middle I opened the door slowly.

My right hand concealed behind my back, psyched up for a knife-hand blow against the throat.

A statuesque, athletic blond stood in front of the door, dressed in jeans, a white T-shirt stretched tightly over her ample bosom. I bit my lip, blocking the Otrera greeting.

She pushed me aside and glided without explanation into the room.

She scanned the room, opened the fridge, looked me up and down, kicked the clotted towel under the bed with an accusing glance before she sat down on the chair, crossing her long spider legs.

Her Amazonian presence filled the room, I opened the window for fresh air and stuck my head outside. I took a deep breath.

'And who the fuck are you?' I asked, conscious of the temporary dip in my vocabulary, but my head was thick, I took an inner oath to stay clear of alcohol for a long time, I did not look at her, the question posed to the sweet tasting, warm afternoon breeze drifting through the concrete jungle.

I turned around.

Her ice cool blue eyes gripped mine. Her tongue

flickered over her lips.

A sardonic smile unfolded around her full mouth, but it did not reach her eyes.

'So, Kaner du Preez,' she over pronounced my name slowly, her Afrikaans accent heavy, 'at last we meet. The files spoke highly of you, the men expect much of you. I have been curious, your file photos do you no justice.'

Her gaze swept over my body and halted on my crotch.

'So, I could not wait to meet you, the white assassin, top of his class, absorbing, passing exams, Angel of Death, the Dark Matter, cold, without emotion, but a dream at the same time, do you know what they call you, the Beautiful Nightmare, one you wish never to have, for the experience is short-lived. How many notches have you carved onto your handmade silver syringe handles? They say you never talk much, claiming to have terminated only one life, can't you remember, what else have they programmed you with, you only react to the one voice calling the command of kill Karelia, the voice of your adopted father, oops, did I say something you did not know?

'Don't say oops, it ruins your carefully cultivated tough cookie image.'

Her face remained nonplussed.

'They say, and boy, Voortrekkerhoogte is rife with rumours and whispers about you and your brother, they say, men cannot resist you, what is it, what is your secret, Angel of Death? What did the foreign legion men teach you in the secret desert camp?'

'To be comprehend the needs of men better than a woman?'

Her laugh bitter, forced.

'Oh, raising your tail now?'

She stood up and crossed the floor.

I craned my neck looking up at her. She was fast, I grant her that, faster than an Egyptian cobra.

I did not flinch as the sharp blow hit the side of my face, the hidden blade in the thumb ring sliced into the upper layers of my skin.

Warm blood trickled down my face. I reeled back. My body tensed.

'Captain Lisa de Villiers, glad to make your acquaintance. You are now in my sector, from the look on your face I can tell you were not warned, Vera did not inform you, good.'

She sat down.

My face stung.

I remained motionless.

Assessing.

Evaluating.

Rummaging through the chronicles of my mind, filing, registering.

Not touching the blood trickle. Watching, learning the world of women.

'Now you listen to me, this is not the bush, nor your training camp with guards protecting you, your lieutenant and general holding your hand and your penis, from what I hear. You are in the viper's nest. Your new friends will slit your throat with the blink of an eye. They did so without blinking over the last twelve months. God knows why they sent a toddler, once again, I will do it with the greatest of pleasures. Did you feel cosy last night, the white filling in the brown sandwich.

Dancing with that despicable woman, touching her buttocks, enthralled by Mother Abishag Africa. Oh, we know she is here, we watched her every move. You drank too much and you took whatever it is you assassin boys take for the kill. Where you planning a kill?' I shook my head.

'You know the rules, no drinking on a mission. The elimination of your target has been brought forward, we have reason to believe Julius will escape the country, disappeared to organise training camps. Salvador-Arano is an unknown to us. A silent killer with a global record. Do not underestimate him, you have youth, he has experience. Stop sniffing around him. We do not know why he is here, he is a disguise master, he vanishes without trace, if he is here to get Julius out of the country, we do not know, we suspect he is here to kill our Prime Minister, head of intelligence, the Boss, you? Sleep with him, pillow talk him. We need a report urgently, if he refuses to divulge information, kill him remotely, not in the city, no doubt he has a tail, guardians from the KGB, perhaps the Chinese Secret Service. He is too valuable an asset, like you are to us. In the mountain you will be on your own. No protection. No safeguard. Any questions?'

I shook my head.

'Julius will take you to his village, I will organise it, the tribals are easy to manipulate. His grandfather will die tonight, heart attack, go with him to the funeral, watch your back, watch Salvador-Arana, you are not a torero, stop playing with him, you can sleep with him, lucky boy, but he is married, but by all accounts you know your way through a ring, no matter how tight.'

She winked.

Captain Lisa de Villiers stood up.

Her cool fingers stroked the red marks on my face, then she disappeared from the room.

I sat down on the bed and laid back, closed my eyes, regurgitating the conversation in my head, dissecting, assigning actions, filing for future reference. I put my trainers on and went for a run.

The city streets were quiet and deserted, shoppers returning laden with bags, a few cars, pigeon flocks flying around aimlessly. Dora nowhere in sight.

Captain Lisa de Villiers sat on a bench in the park, smoke spiralled from the cigarette she held in a cigarette holder.

Her eyes followed me as I jogged down the path and the water.

No musicians today. I disappeared between the tall, concrete buildings, a slow, oppressive heat radiated from the tarmac underneath my feet.

I kept running, increasing my speed, desert trained, numb to my environment.

His whispering voice urging me on.

'Kill Karelia kill.'

## *Township butterfly flutterings!*

The smoke hung low over the rows and rows of corrugated iron shacks. It was a warm summer afternoon, yet fires burned in drums, sending black smoke into the already saturated smoggy air.

Where drums could not be obtained, old motor tires were set alight, it was with relief I noticed the tire fires were not used for cooking meat, only meeting places for young black men and women gathering in intimate circles of conversation.

There were few old people on the street. It was ten past seven, the remains of the day visible in the sky, soon it would be dark. Yesterday I noticed in this eastern part of the country the sun set rapidly, no long drawn out sunsets, the final brush of the sky rapid, fast, like the captain's hand.

The same moon rising over Norway, sat heavy and

low in the dawn sky.

I sat next to Salvador-Arana.

He looked very handsome in his dark blue V-neck sweater. I fixed my eyes on him for a while. His beautiful bone structure.

His voice, mellow, softly spoken. He had such style and grace.

I was so curious about him, and felt a certain thrill sitting next to him.

It all felt rather grown-up, as if I had a date on a Saturday evening, with a man from over the seas, how utterly wicked in its delectableness.

The handsome Argentinian collected me from a street corner nearby the Hanging Tree.

A dangerous rendezvous point as I had no idea who watched me and who followed me. By then I was certain words about my presence in the City of Gold spread like a Hollywood wild fire.

There was no doubt in my mind, the international intelligence and counterterrorism communities treated my mission with the same caution as if the Russians launched their submarines and ballistic missile-crews in the direction of America.

I could have done with one of my bleak, endlessly White Russian cocktails.

I winked at Captain Lisa before I climbed in the car. She sat like a comma queen on her moped. Her legs swinging and her arms hanging loose. Before I got ready, I did some admin work.

I had eight hundred and fifty emails to check. I used the chair and bed and fridge to do some weight training, then further admin.

Then back to weight training.

I thought to run out and look for Zumba classes, but at the last minute decided against it.

Once we pulled away from the kerb, I dared not looking back, for fear of attracting unwanted suspicion. If ever there was time I need to keep myself übercool like Naomi Campbell, it was now.

I recalled Naomi once said she understood from a very early age what it meant to be black. She had to be twice as good.

The same applied to me now. I was a fully fledge spy now. I had to be thrice as good if I ever wanted to stand a chance being signed up with an international spy agency.

I was not sure if I was followed, I dared not look back as we drove through the streets of downtown City of Gold, through the southern suburbs and onto the poorly maintained road towards Soweto.

I felt calm in the beauteous evening. It felt natural sitting next to this hunk.

My mind was clear like mountain water streaming down the hills.

So were my veins.

The admin, weight training and two hour run through the city suburbs like a mole on a quick overground patrol around the ant's nests perked me up.

I suspect the hand of the captain had brought me back to reality. Salvador-Arano raised an quizzical eyebrow at the cut but chose to say nothing.

Jogging through the streets earlier in the afternoon, I reflected on the last twenty four hours in the city, the ease with which Julius and Salvador-Arano permitted my entrance into their circle.

Did they have suspicions?

Who was the real bait?

The voice within advised I could take care of myself, even amongst the highly rated enemy.

We passed yellow police vans along the way.

I lowered in the passenger seat, di the law prohibited white people going into black townships, was I suppose to carry a pass, was I permitted here, did white people venture into the servant quarters?

Father Isaac forbade me.

On the farm I never visited the coloureds at their homes, Mama never permitted it, maybe on the orders of Grandma Esther, or Father Isaac.

I walked into Dina's room in our backyard a few times, the smells strange, enticing and repulsive at the same time, sweet vaseline mixed with burned hair.

Once I walked in, unannounced, catching Dina in the act of ironing her hair. She pulled an iron comb, heated on the primus stove, through her hair, the stench nauseatingly repulsive.

I left quietly so as not to offend her. Through the window I watched her rubbing Vaseline onto the ironed hair. Tears dripped from her eyes.

During supper I watched her touched her burned scalp several times.

Poor Dina.

Mama reprimanded her for touching her scalp whilst serving us food.

'It is not easy being a non-white,' I thought.

We drove in an old Ford Mustang, gold coloured, rather awful, leather seats torn, the radio-cassette player broken.

The Argentinian was chatty for the first twenty minutes, then focused on the road.

I took in the landmarks as we moved forward into the unknown world of black suburban living. Lonely, starved dogs wandered the streets in packs, little boys kicking balls.

A contrast to the white suburbs, where children seldom played in streets, here the black children were out in force. Space in the shacks was limited, no doubt living conditions were crammed, extended families huddled together.

'Like rats,' the General said, 'they keep breeding, with nowhere to live, unbelievable, we will never understand, trying to outnumber us in the numbers game.'

Water ran down the streets from taps. Mud puddles formed, trampled through by man and animal.

It was a strange world, foreign, not quite magical, but with a dreamlike quality, black and grey dreams, shanty world colours. Salvador-Arano stopped the car under a disused bridge, grown over, nature reclaiming the human footprints.

A lonely, faded caravan parked underneath. One window broken. The door flung open.

A thin black woman stepped outside, made her way over to the fire burning in the tin where she turned the meat over, and sat down on a worn out, green canvas chair. She looked tired.

The purple head scarf sat askew as she scratched her head with one index finger. Round green beads drooped from her ears.

She drank from a glass jar and looked up when we climbed out of the car. Her eyes followed our movements. No recognition flickered as she watched Salvador-Arana, I deduced this was his first visit too.

'Julius,' she shouted into the caravan door opening, the remainder of her monologue in an African language I did not understand.

Julius appeared in the caravan door. He looked different, serious, a smile briefly lit his handsome black face. White teeth aligned.

I ran my tongue over my teeth, they were not so tidily arranged. He greeted Salvador-Arano in a brotherly hug, I was welcomed with an outstretched handshake, not quite the same welcome, he appeared less jovial towards me than last, or was it me being neurotic, looking for signals, but of what, foe or friend?

The voice whispering in the recesses of my mind.

'Come into my humble abode, this is my auntie Josephine.'

A black hand held out, hard, dry skin pressed against mine.

'Auntie worked all day in Sandton as a maid for white people. She arrived home an hour ago, I appreciate you cooking for us, Auntie.'

Auntie reached out and touched his leg.

'Have you been in a township before Kaner?'

We sat down on oil drums around Auntie. Four scraggly dogs sauntered up the dusty road and joined our company.

'First time, its different, rugged, mysterious,' I replied, which was true, there was something about this place, 'It has character, it feels everyone belongs here, together.'

I was not sure my answer was correct, but decided it was best to speak my mind.

Julius and Auntie laughed heartily.

'Well, we sure belong here, courtesy of your people, by day we are allowed to dwell on the shiny floors of the white homes, by night we are banished to the cold cement floors and muddy streets of this.'

Julius waved his hand in the direction of the streets, his laughter turned bitter, the last few words spoken harshly.

He leaned forward.

'This has to end Kaner, your people has to stop suppressing my people, you invaded our land like termites, arriving in large swarms on our continent, a continent you white people left in search of greener pastures. Now you infested the fibre of African society, forming new societies, too lazy to feed yourselves, subjecting us to life as slaves, your soldiers terminating us, just because of the colour of our skin.'

His voice rose as he spoke, passion spilling into the dust.

His black hand gripped my wrist. I looked down at the black hand resting on my white skin.

I surprised myself at the queer calmness I felt. If we were alone, I would have strangled him right here and now for his arrogance in the touching of me.

The law of the land remain the law of the land, even in the township. This was not a night club, but open air street reality. This was exactly what the General referred to. Insolence.

'Give them your pinky and they will swallow your arm.' This was not my time, this was his time. Let him hang himself, give him rope.

Auntie laid a hand on Julius.

209

'Be kind to our guest.' Julius sat back.

'Sorry,' he mumbled. He disappeared into the caravan.

A fridge door opened creakily.

He appeared with cans of soft drinks. Silence prevailed.

Nearby laughter drifted into our circle.

Auntie turned the meat. The dogs watched her every movement, willing her with droopy eyes to acknowledge their presence.

'They killed his childhood friend some time ago, Temba,' she said, looking at me, 'the most innocent boy nature created. A harmless creature, four fingers.'

Auntie tapped her index fingers and thumbs against each other.

'They grew up together as herd boys. Then one day, Temba disappeared, kidnapped, sold as a boy soldier, he joined the resistance movement, in his own special way he contributed to the fight for our people, until they,' her voice hardened, 'the pigs, tracked him down, killed him, he who had no defence, he who was the friend of butterflies, not a fly he would hurt, they burned his body. Left his ashes for the wind to scatter. Another restless soul of an African child dwelling eternally across Africa.'

Auntie stood up. Her lanky figure towered above us. She pulled her headscarf off. Her head criss-crossed with scars. She grabbed Julius's hand.

'You must find the murderer of my sister's child, set his soul free so he can rest in peace. I can not meet my sister in the afterlife, if you, who I raised as my own, has not fulfilled his duty. Show the white pig no mercy when you found him.'

She sat down, bowed her head for a moment, before serving the meat on paper plates. Julius brought bread rolls out.

We ate in silence.

I could not help starring at the scars. I was dying to know, but decided it was probably best not to ask right now.

Julius put more logs in the tin, flames flicked above the rim. Darkness descended onto the small group of four people gathered under the bridge.

A small world in a large troubled continent. The dogs gnawed noisily on the bones thrown in their direction. It was the first time I had eaten with black people. How different was this world.

Was I sinning?

Was I disobedient to my people. Questions raced through my head.

I wanted to know more about Temba. Did Julius suspect who I was, or was I here because the General knew, was this the reason I was sent to kill Julius and not cousin Alex?

'We must go shortly, the people are waiting,' Julius said as soon as we cleared the plates. It was the tastiest chicken meat I ate in a long time. I thanked Auntie for the food. She smiled.

'You are welcome child, do come back anytime.' She clapped both hands in my direction.

'Now before you boys go, I will be asleep by the time you get back, if you do, for surely, you young men, with fire in your blood, will not seek the comfort of your beds on a Saturday night, you must warm the heart of a woman with a full belly, with a few sounds. You have your guitar in the car, Guapo? Play me the sounds of your faraway land, warm my blood so I can dream the dreams of a young maiden on a Saturday night, alone in my bed.'

'Si Mamita.'

Salvador-Arano stood up and walked to the car. He returned with his guitar.

He sat down on the steps of the caravan and stroked the strings. Rich guitar sounds drifted into the night. Julius leaned back in his chair and lit a cigarette.

He blew thin smoke circles.

His eyes veiled. The mask of Africa, emotions hidden, thoughts secret, I could not detect a single emotion, a thought process, a hint of his assessment of the moment. I did not dare rest my gaze on him too long.

Auntie stood up and stomped her feet on the dusty earth and clapped her hands above her head, fusing African and Argentinian beats.

The dogs scattered into the safety of the night, the ones not able to rescue their bones, barked half-heartedly and glared back at the humans.

Auntie's face gleamed in the fire, a faint glimpse of the woman she was, when the three men around her were still toddling.

She grabbed me and I fell in with her beat. We danced, clapped hands and laughed.

I twirled Auntie a few times, adding my down dance style to her blend. Salvador-Arano played faster and faster, every now and then, he lifted his hand from the strings and beat the rhythm on the guitar box.

Faster and faster, until Auntie and I fell down exhaustedly in the dust.

She planted a kiss on my lips. The music stopped.

'You boys are a tonic for an old lady. Go, go, before I lock you three in the caravan with me.' Julius stood up. With great reverence he bent over and kissed the woman on her forehead.

'Ulale kahle, Umamkhulu,' he bade her goodnight.

I took her hand and kissed it.

'Ngiyabonga kakhulu, you city people know how to have fun, one day I will come back and tell you a story, you give me three words, and I will weave you a tapestry of life.'

Salvador-Arano asked me to hold his guitar as he pressed the slender female body close to his, kissed her on the neck and stood up.

He looked down at her with an intensity I have not seen up to now.

'Mamita, I will kill the cojones, who brought the sadness to your family, with my bare hands, I promise you.'

She smiled, nodded and whispered a barely audible, 'Ngiyabonga Indonana, may the spirit of the dead have mercy on the incarnation of forbidden love.'

An owl, disturbed from its early sleep, fluttered from under the bridge, stuttering a bubbling series of po's-po's. Orange eyes gleaming in the white face. A ominous shudder ran down my legs. I shivered.

Salvador-Arano placed his arm around my shoulder and pulled me close to him.

He planted a kiss on my neck. His breath warm, quelling the chill down my spine.

I did not doubt the sincerity of his words. How much did he know? Would he make the first move? I relaxed into the arm around my shoulder.

This man was more sensitive than the men I'd met to date. He was danger, I felt a stirring in my groin, a warmth seeping.

The white-faced owl perched on a high wire, inspecting the intruders. Salvador-Arano crossed himself.

'Are you superstitious,' I asked.

'Survival sharpens nature's senses, ask any peasant.'

Auntie Josephine remained on the steps as we drove off, the dogs slinked back to her, she cut a lonely figure in front of the caravan under the bridge.

### *Nothing was the same!*

The streets were busy, young and old walked up and down the dusty streets.

Faint candle and paraffin lights burned in windows, electricity was not on offer, nor was running water, only from the free flowing streets taps.

If it was not for the poverty, the scene greeting my eyes could have been romantic, another world co-existing with the one I knew so well, I felt comfortable, this was closer to desert life than the flat in Joubert Park, the cement buildings and streets filled with parked cars man-made, unnatural.

Here fires burned, groups of people huddled around the fire, waving and shouting in at the car as we drove along, throwing curious looks at the white passengers. Julius was a well-known and respected figure.

The flames glowed eerily over the low hung smog

stage. It was Saturday night. Kwela and pop music drifted through the car windows.

The yellow full moon suspended low. Moonlit silhouettes led our way. A shooting star arched through the sky.

'Make a wish, ' I said to Salvador-Arana.

'Being here is a wish come true,' he replied, closing his eyes for a few seconds, 'just made another one.'

We stopped at a darkened house. A red brick house. No fence. No grass. No trees. No shrubs. A solitary home. Blinds pulled down. Two fires burned on either side of the entrance door in pits dug into the ground.

We walked up a well trodden path.

Julius greeted people along the way. They returned his greeting respectful, in the manner of the Hanging Tree people.

'Po-po-po.'

An owl perched on the tin roof edge. We followed Julius into the house. Salvador-Arano and I were the only white people in the room. People milled around, glasses in the hand, an eclectic mix of black people sat on worn out sofas, perched on arm rests, leant against walls, glasses filled with amber coloured liquids in their hands, a jovial atmosphere with underlying tones of political seriousness, African languages interspersed with English phrases and fragments, bodies swaying to seductive middle eastern dance beats. Introductions made on the way in.

'Tabo Mshalanga, editor, Morning Soweto, Kaner, Salvador-Arana.' We shook hands. Foe of the state, a thorn in the flesh of the government.

'Thembi Tshabalala, president, Youth League.' She

kissed us on the cheek. A face I recognised, trouble, instigator.

'Dali Mashonga, actor.' We shook hands. Blown-up posters with black freedom fighter faces on the walls guarded over proceedings, I recognised Steve Biko and stopped at a photo of a familiar looking man.

'Madiba,' Julius whispered. What? A photo of the most dangerous man in the country, banished to the island of the Mother City. A young man's grainy face, the only picture existing of him. Photos of ageing black resistance leaders were not on display in the history books of white children. It was not in our interests.

'A life sentence served on our father and his brothers as you took your first steps Karelia.' His eyes dead as he whispered the words intimately into my ears. Ice bear fingers clawed around my heart. I willed my heartbeat down, reliving the excruciating beating on my broken fingers, 'you feel nothing, you float, you feel nothing.'

Julius did his homework. His moves on the chessboard calculated. I was no longer in doubt, the warnings of Vera and the captain sounded. A Che Guevara poster added colour to the room. Silence hushed as we reached the front of the room.

I sat down in the front row on a wooden chair with no arm rests. I counted seventy people crammed into the room, seated, standing. The atmosphere electrified. Strange human body odours tickled my nose. Salvador-Arana's presence comforting.

Young men dressed in black military uniforms closed the front door and locked it, guarding over entrance and departure. Guards took up position in front of the blinded windows. No entry or exit permitted. The house was in session.

Julius re-appeared wearing a beret and dark sunglasses. Flanked by six body guards he strolled down the aisle with an air of authority. The guards lined up behind him at the front of the room. At the back of the room someone flicked a switch. A spot light lit up the speaker, his presence superior.

His voice masterful. I cold, dead inside. My instincts washed over me. My arms hung loosely at my side. The scorpion waiting guardedly.

'My beloved comrades, I welcome you on this special night, hidden from the eyes of the world. Sentries are posted, alert to the arrival of the yellow vans. Tonight I welcome two illustrious guests from different part of the worlds we inhabit. One of them lived through the revolution, the other one is almost desperately trying to stem the revolution tide in our country. One a friend, one a foe,' he said.

'I trust one. I despised one. A friend and a traitor. A scorching sun and an ice cool moon. Balance is required in nature. This evening I embraced both of them in an expression of my reverie and hatred. One spilled tears of friendship on my chest, the other, a cytotoxic adder, coiled, its fangs retracted, waiting for the moment to catch its prey off guard, and release its deadly venom, like a female adder he releases pheromones to attract his victims, penetrating the soft layers of belly skin.'

My body stayed taut, I focused on slowing my heartbeat, prevention of tiny sweat-beads breaking out on the forehead was key.

Julius stopped, his dark glasses focused on his guests, but who?

Unable to second guess his stare, I locked eyes with the black mirrors above his nose. The white-faced owl uttered a series of fast, bubbling hoots from somewhere outside in the night under the yellow full moon. The silence in the room deafening, the owl wings fluttering drifting through the corrugated iron roof.

'Darkness wandered through the portal of his veins, not even the angels dare to tread for fear of walking in the presence of the Angel of Death.'

Julius slowly raised a fisted left arm. His arm stopped mid-air, the fist unfolded slowly, an index finger rose up, thumb folded in, joining the three remaining fingers in a semi-fist, an accusing finger directed at my heart.

Iron arms clasped my wrists behind the chair.

My neck grappled in a full nelson, brutal pressure cranked my neck immobile, a blinding pain shot through my body, my body unable to pull away.

A hand jerked my head upwards, forceful as it demanded I face their leader.

I relaxed into the grip, willing emotions from my being. The smell drifting up from the black skin repulsed me.

'Thief of the night. Under the cloak of the dark this scorpion sneaked from the warmth of the desert sand with an erected stinger to mate and terminate. Hunting down his victims with care. The white pig transmuted into a dark creature of the night. Killing our beloved Themba, my childhood friend. Shall I have mercy on his soul?'

'No,' the voices behind me cried in unison.

'Shall I revenge the death our beloved scorpion boy, a freedom fighter lost forever?'

'Yes.'

'To set his soul free from roaming aimlessly, let it find

peace amongst our ancestors and illustrious warriors of the past?'

The audience hissed their approval.

Chairs pushed aside scraped the floor as they thrust forward, lining up behind my chair.

Their body heat overwhelming, their hatred overpowering.

'Kill the Boer, kill the Boer, kill the Boer,' they chanted, the golden veneer of elegant city people sanded from the surface, centuries old ingrained hatred released, the face of Africa revealed, acting in accord with their environment, town ship people ready to be shipped out into the slave plantations of the world.

God, why did we have mercy on them for so long. Julius stepped forward, his breath warm in my face.

A black briefcase held open, he reached in and removed a black scorpion mask which he placed over my head. With a fell swoop he ripped my T-shirt open, undo my belt and ripped my jeans and underwear off.

I stood naked. My vision restricted by two slits in the mask.

'Is he a man?'

Laughter around me.

'Let him look in the mirror, let the scorpion see himself, he who dared to sting the butterfly. Look at him now, his stinger devoid of venom. I will kill him with his eyes wide shut.'

He held a mirror in front of my face. I stared at a grotesque spider face with the bluest eyes hidden behind malicious slits. Mama's words rang in my head.

'They think they can kill us. Our black skins they will never trust, they who turned their backs on us, on our

Mother Africa. Bayete! He will not beg, his heart is frozen, a black maggot filled hole devoured his soul long before his departure from the womb, my spear I will thrust through his hear tonight, setting the soul of my childhood friend free.'

His commanding voice no longer was controlled, it was the voice of a mad man, possessed, dangerous, not in control of himself, devoid of all human emotions, filled with revengeful thoughts.

He face he pressed up rather overbearingly close to my delicate features.

No kindness displayed in his soul. His eyes shone with brilliant madness.

'What do you have to say to yourself white boy?' he hissed.

'Stay calm, say nothing, if you loose control, you loose the battle,' the voice of the General resonated in my head.

In my mind yellow-brown leaves fell from the semi-barren winter trees readying themselves for their extended nodding off. Burnt copper splashes against a grey wintery sky.

'Outstare your enemy, outwit your enemy, unnerve him,' Moshe's advice clashed with the older guard's. I succumbed to my own will. 'End my life at your peril, my soul will not rest, I will come back to haunt you Kaf...'

Next thing the idiot rose his two fists in the air. I saw them come forward and tried to shrank back.

If he wanted to see fear in my eyes, he was going to wait until Moses' ark descended back from Mars to where the aliens took it for examination of human history.

'I could kill you,' he said. He choked with rage, scarce able to breath.

'You best do it, if not, I'll kill you the moment your monkeys take their stinky hands of my lily-white skin, you piece of filth,' I said, 'and by God, I would do just that.'

His eyes glared at me. Not a grain of physical fear showed in mine, or so I bleedin' hope. Julius glared around, was he bewildered.

Then his face exploded into the mask.

My head snapped back. I tasted blood and spit and skin inside my mouth.

I bit my tongue to still the pain I felt in my head. The idiot lost control. Just what I wanted.

I was gratified to see thin black eyebrows drawn up in a sort of peevish misery.

I always thought black don't crack, but this one cracked in front of my eyes and his mates like a piece of cheap water bottle plastic.

I strained against the black steel muscle rods. They did not relent.

Next thing a knee sank into my cocoanuts. Bastards! That fucking hurt.

Now of course I screamed that in my head. There was no fucking way I'll let on the pain I suffered in my crown jewels box.

After-all, this was not a peep-show.

'Good evening,' I said with clenched teeth, 'so now you freedom fucking dumbwaiter morons want to play dirty. Suck my dick if you are man enough. Don't fucking ruin my nuts. Come one, this is suppose to be a gentleman's game, or what?'

Someone forcibly ejected saliva as a gesture of their contempt for me by spitting on me.

Or perhaps I gave the imbeciles a hard one once they saw my impressive bulge.

I saw Julius rubbed his head.

A lanky fella handed him a syringe which Julius held in front of my face. Tiny droplets overflow from the top.

'Your own medicine Child Killer,' he said.

Pale liquid squirted from the needle.

I readied myself, yanked my head in the direction of Salvador-Arana, would he show me mercy, would he hold my head on his lap and tell me a story?

I decided to change tactic.

My eyes implored the indecipherable message in his dark Argentinian eyes.

I looked down.

The needle glided into the soft folds of my stomach.

Then the prick - not half bad.

At least no agonising pain jolted through my body. Probably a fucking bloody placebo.

Amateurs!

The last face I stared at, before the black oblivion washed over me, was a black face, oh darn the cruelty of life.

I closed my eyes behind the scorpion mask.

A crack opened in my mind and down my spirit flowed.

## *The Brotherhood of Men!*

The sky was a ghostly blue. The moon hung low, lower than the mountain peak I stood upon. The moon surface filled with craters, growth like a walrus overgrown with algae. A shadow floated across the silver blue water but there was no movement detectable in the water.

I looked around for a sign of life, all was quiet, not a breeze, not a ripple, no fluttering of wings. I waited, I always waited, knowing it would come.

Had I died, arrived alone at the valley of death?

The sky emptied of stars offered a starless view.

I shivered, how strange, it was not cold, was it fear?

'You do not fear,' I whispered softly to myself.

Then, faintly, in a distance, the fluttering of wings, stronger and stronger.

No sound reached my ears, no drawn out piercing ha-di-da, ha-di-da. It shimmered in the dark, the long wings flapped in slow motion as if tired.

Suspended I hung in the centre of the flightpath.

In horror I recoiled, like a little Lulu bumble bee, her wings paralysed by freezing cold weather.

Carven eyes starred at me, the sockets hollow, the eyes dropped out.

Blood dripped from the wing tips. My childhood friend hurt and blinded. The hadida hovered above me. The underside of its wings coloured a ghostly grey.

'What happened?'

My voice broke free in a bare whisper. In the blue stillness of the night the hadida plumage shone with luminous purple sheen. The fluttering of its wings disturbing the night air and sound silence.

'Did you follow me from Camp Basawa,' I asked. I signalled the bird to land next to me, the hadida clutched its claws and unfolded, clutch and unfolded. Long chains, hooks at the end, lowered from the claws, the noise shattered the silence, disturbing the peace. The hadida turn its head away from me towards the moon. Its beak opened, no sound escaped but a gush of air filled with the decay of rotten flesh.

I reached for the chains, but it swayed from me, it had a life of its own, like the snakes of Medusa.

The hooks tore into my flesh, I felt no pain, where no flesh existed it pierced my body and exited on the other side.

The bird flapped its wings and hoisted me into the sky, up and up and away. We dropped from the mountaintop and lowered over the river.

Small ripples churned up the moon shadow. A long row boat slowly made it way down the river.

Twelve old women with long silvery hair heaved at the oars. They warbled in soprano voices, 'Tonight the sword will kill the Sorcerer, the double edged sword seeks revenge, the worms of decay unleashed in the furnace of hell, a frozen moon hasten the tide, ripping the stars from the sky, as the Nero night darkens the sins of a forgotten child, will the Unicorn come to his aid, a decision only a mother can take.'

At the back of the boat was someone I recognised.

I strained my eyes and yanked at the chains, urging the hadida to lower me. The wings stilled, we glided down.

'Mama,' I screamed, 'Mama, Mama.'

Louder and louder, my presence unacknowledged by her, she did not even look up.

'Go on, you scream, get her attention, they are taking her away from me,' I screamed desperately at the bird.

He opened his mouth, another gush flowed from its beak, adder hissing escaping over the crooked beak.

Fearful I watched the transformation, the bird head altering into a cobra hood.

Two fangs unfolded, silver droplets dripped on me, sergeant snake restored from the dead.

'No, no, God help me, anybody help me, I don't want to die, I am sorry, I am sorry, I just did as I was told, god help me, Mama, Abel, help me.'

The hood swung back, poised to attack.

I folded my arms protectively over my head, a feeble attempt to hide from the onslaught.

I watched in horror as the cobra head lowered itself, a

ruby light glowed deep within the empty sockets, a loud piercing wail escaped my mouth.

I opened my eyes, dazed and confused, slowly taking in my new surroundings.

I laid still, watching the figures around the fire move about. Heads held closed together, voices whispering.

It was dark.

Beyond the human figures loomed huts and trees against the backdrop of a forest covered in a dense fog.

Tiny black children sat in a circle away from the fire.

The fog from the forest had penetrated my head, I kept my breathing low and slow, suppressing the need to call for water, feelings of nausea sloshing around in my stomach.

I was in a village, from the thin mountain air I could tell I was high up in the mountains, where exactly I was not sure, but I had a hunch.

I identified the familiar head shapes of Julius and Salvador-Arana.

Salvador-Arano turned his head around. My reflexes were too slow to avoid his gaze.

He nudged Julius.

'Ah, the Scorpion boy returned from Tophet.'

Black faces with big white eyes turned in my direction. Fire light played across the dark faces, dancing shadows obscuring facial features, stoicism, the mask of Africa's children.

Julius stood up, a leopard clock draped from his shoulders.

I laid motionless, watching the scene from behind the scorpion mask slits.

My hands and feet were untied, I was grateful for the

small tokens of reprieve, as I suddenly realised I was not dead, unless my spirit killed them all and transported the whole lot of us to a mountainous African hell.

It dawned on me, I was in the village of the Scorpion boy, without doubt my killing was top of the agenda, to set the soul of the letter bomb murder free. The soporific effects wore off, I felt relieved.

Did Julius have the courage to revenge the death of his childhood friend and so brought the ancient Zulu curse onto himself?

He did not dare to hand me over to the police or the authorities, as the tradition demanded. This was a catch 22 for him. Urban warrior and traditional values in conflict.

My mind raced through the notes in the folder of Temba.

This must be the village of Lambutshashi, the playground of Uvevane, Fezela Boy.

I forced myself upright.

Slowly, hypnotically I tapped my index fingers against my thumbs, lifting my arms above my head as I did so, following the beat of a lonely drum.

How many of them had ever seen a white man, time ticked slower up here, away from the intruding eyes of people living in cement towers and driving down tarred roads.

A gasp rose from the group assembled around the fire.

A few elders stood up and sank down on their knees in reverie.

The children stopped playing, their attention turned to the fire.

The dogs raised their heads, aware something was about to happen, the stray cats watched me with big black eyes.

I raised from the floor, improvising a dance as I did so, instincts in control, knowing the African myth for half human, half animal creatures their sky goddesses gave birth to, creatures inheriting the earthly spirit of an animal.

I danced the chi wara ton with the scorpion mask on, conscious the faces staring at me would recognise the tribal believes of the continental tribes.

Julius suspected my game.

He grabbed a beer calabash and walked over to me, forcing my mouth open, pouring a bitter-sweet tasting liquid down my throat.

I spluttered, his exploding fist in my stomach forced my mouth open as he jerked my head back and poured more liquid down my throat.

I swallowed, quenching my thirst, mixing the village beer with the narcotic aftereffects.

He ripped the mask from my face.

I continued my dance, four fingers tapping in the air. Julius grabbed my hand, with lightening speed he pulled his knife from his pocket and cut the index finger from my left hand off in a single fell swoop.

I groaned and fell to the ground, clutching my hand as I watched in horror Julius holding the cut finger above his head.

A gasp escaped from the audience at this macabre spectacle.

A shadow fell over the gathering.

A grotesque naked figure stepped in from the

shadows, large breasts wobbled ahead of the oversized, multilayered fat human being. Her face painted white, a headdress of feathers adorned her head. Two black mambas rested their flat heads on the ample chest, motionless, their slitty black eyes keeping careful watch of the human gathering. Tongues flickering restless.

The sangoma duck-walked in my direction.

I slowly moved away from her, my childhood snake fear stirring in my toes.

This was not the time for irrational dislikes butI did not trust myself.

My head felt heady from the sorghum. The amputated throbbing pain surged through body.

Desperately I attempted stemming the blood flow by pressing my right hand over the stub.

The sangoma turned her back on me.

A butterfly cloak hung from her back.

Julius whispered into her ear. The sangoma reached into the leather pouch covering her vagina.

She pulled a handful of white powder out which she threw into the fire.

A loud hissing sound exploded as white smoke billowed up. She threw her head back, a wild howl noise escaped from her throat.

The drum beat stopped, silence descended on the forest, nature and humans holding their breaths.

Then a fluttering, softly at first, slowly increasing in volume, louder and louder.

All eyes turned to the forest where the noise was coming from.

The only one not watching was the witch woman. She stood with her eyes closed, her hands held up in the sky, her body shaking, the snakes lifted their heads into her face, forked tongues flickering over her face, sensing her, touching her.

From the forest thousands of yellow and back butterflies flew over the village, their tiny shadows crawling over the ground.

The Viceroys in full flight. On their faces not funny notions, nor smiling notions, not oops, not whoops, like little boys in the corner, the butterflies casted second glances in my direction. Glances I in the years to follow treasured during the long dark hours of my banishment to that island in the middle of an hostile in coldness island.

The villagers fell down to the ground, whimpering, praying, letting the butterfly swarm wash over them.

With no eyes on me, I moved swiftly to the sangoma, placed my hand behind the hand of the mamba and ripped one from her neck. She opened her eyes,  dark eyes meeting mine, she said nothing.

The snake coiled in my hand, lashing its thick body around my arm. Its head sparked left, then right. I avoided eye contact with the evil eyes, so unkind in nature.

I sprinted away from the fire into the butterfly cloud, heading towards the forest. The tiny butterfly figures fluttered around, obscuring views. Butterfly phlegm obscured my path. Some of them, like me, cocoon released too soon.

The sky filled with butterflies.

Rhopalocerous.

Papilionaceous.

Rhopaloceral

The sound of feet behind me. Blood dripped onto my feet. Silent amoroso dins too silent.

I glanced over my shoulder, it was Julius.

I increased my speed, I reached the dense vegetation, keeping the aggressive open stretched mamba mouth away from my body.

I dared not look at the inky black mouth, venom dripping from the fangs, a strike now would be lethal. The strong muscles pressing forcefully in an attempt to arch its back.

Essex skipper.

Camberville beauty.

Granville fritillary

I kept the my finger stub in my mouth, pressing my tongue against the raw flesh, tasting my blood, swallowing it, feeling invigorated, feeding myself, keep myself alive.

The forest was quiet, holding its breath, nocturnal life watching from secret towers the human drama unfolding. I slowed down, listening to the nearing footsteps.

Queen of Spain.

Duke of Burgundy.

Cleopatra.

At last a level playing ground.

I felt dizzy. Vulnerable. My innocence short lived. My fate entwined with that of the young black man.

Time to execute.

'Kill Karelia kill,' forest whispers urged me, even the snake relaxed in my grip, sensing my senses, anticipated the soft skin to sink their fangs into.

Lallygag.

Baisrmain.

Butterfly kisses.

Carefree. Smiling. Handholding

Red admiral.

Peacock.

Hermit.

Time to kill.

I stepped into a clear spot.

A single branched tree reached up in the sky, its leafless branches ghostly reaching into all four directions of the wind.

Fingers reaching out.

The moonlight bathed my naked body in silver. I held the snake at arms length, slowing my breath, dropping my pulse rate, tensing each muscle, my body was alert, poised, in position to rear, to strike.

The familiar fire stirring in my groin, wiping out fear, obliterating pain.

Julius stepped into the moonlit circle. I leaned back against the tree, arching my back, thrusting my pelvis forward, my manhood raising its head.

My intention clear and on display. He watched me intently, stepping forward with caution, not sure what to make of the finger sucking man with a snake in his hand.

I smelled his uncertainty, his curiosity, his animalistic instinct, the throw of the dice.

I removed my hand from my mouth.

I stroke myself with four fingers and a bleeding stub, inviting my enemy into my sanctuary, into my lair, promising his seclusion, enjoyment, transmitting the call of nature, man against man.

Nothing to distract us now.

Only the two of us and nature. Words not required, basic human instincts at play, in command, both of us answering the call of nature, live or die. Male primeval desires coming out to play.

The black man stopped two footsteps from me.

His fists curled up at his sides, his eyes seeking reassurance in mine.

I willed him to trust me, to follow his desires.

He loosened his jeans and cloak.

My eyes dropped to the black manhood, proud and erected it reached out in the dark, pining.

I reached out for him, guiding, coaching him. He stepped forward, his exposed helmet gleaming in the moonlight.

I touched him gently with my fingertips.

His penis moved smoothly into my open palm, resting, nestling.

My fingers wrapped firmly around the firm, thick African girth.

Warm blood pulsating through a vein, resting in my warm blood, the blood of proud Zulu warriors who once roamed these hills with murderous lust in their groins.

I held the snake at bay.

His eyes closed with the caressing touch.

Our manhoods met, sniffing at each other, exploring, both pulsating.

I pulled him closer, his body radiated warmth, sensuality, small sweat beads rolling down his forehead.

I breathed deeper, urging him on with sensual breathing.

Time stood still in the forest, not a sound, not a whisper, two men suspended in time as ancient ingrained desires raced through their veins, giving themselves over to primitive drives, compulsions, here man made laws did not apply, only instincts, natural, yearned for.

I increased the pressure on the adder head, forcing the mouth open.

A soft hiss escaped from deep within the coiled body. The black man opened its lips, ready to kiss me, ready to meet a white boy's tongue.

I manoeuvred the snake head closer to the body, calculating each movement with vigilant care, one slip and my life will be taken from me by both aborigines.

I jerked Julius forward by his penis, his soft tummy skin rammed gently into the waiting fangs as I took a step to the right, the honed fangs piercing the skin with ease.

The snake throat pulsated as it pumped deadly venom into the soft human folds, it had exceptionally long venom glands, I massaged the muscles hard, emptying the poison chambers.

I sidestepped the African curse, letting nature executed natural justice, let it not be said this black man died at my hand.

Julius stepped back, his eye opened in shocked disbelief, slowly fear crept in as reality sank in, again and again.

I repeatedly emptied the deadly venom into his bloodstream, forcing the snake to bite and bite, I sank its fangs into his stomach, heart, and face repeatedly.

I buried my bloody stub deep into his left eye, driving the eyeball back into its socket, weakening the curse of the dying man's eyes.

The youthful face distorted in horror as the toxins interfered with his bodily functions, his fighting spirit paralysed as the viper venom overdose decimated his peripheral nervous system.

Neurotoxins tamed his manhood, now drooping limply.

I tossed the snake aside, exhausted and with emptied chambers the serpent slithered cowardly away, relieved to escape from the hand of man and human dramas it did not understood, an innocent bystander.

My own manhood stood proud as my target dropped to his knees. The powerful warrior defeated at my feet.

I crouched over, cradling his head in my lap, huddling his head close to the warmth of my body.

He jolted, his eyes silently interviewing me, his black skin pale and grey.

I pushed the eye lids closed as the sightless eyeball of the sun sunk low behind the horizon.

'I don't want to die,' Julius whispered.

Dark red blood ran in rivulets down his mouth corners, the poison denuding his intestines.

I ran my stub over his lips, our black and white blood amalgamating in the last hours of his life, his lips painted red, the warrior prepared for his arrival in the netherworld, for I had no doubt, his spirit would leave this world to join the army of kings, long gone, engaged in the eternal battles of good and evil, for if peace is not made in this world, then surely the battle rages on in the life we inherit once departed.

'Shhh, I know, I know, no one wants to die,' I quietened him, 'don't talk, let go, listen to the wind rustling through the trees, it calls you to the land far away, where your spirit will roam freely over the grassland along with the spirit of a brave lion, don't fear death, cross the threshold brave warrior where your ancestors await your arrival. Look up, see the mist, it's the spirits of your ancestors, awaiting you, welcoming you. There, look, it's Thembo, your childhood friend, he is smiling,  looking forward to your arrival, go now, brave warrior, your time is over. Once upon a time three warthogs decided they wished to see what lies on the land where the sun rises every day.....'

I crossed his arms over his chest, his skin cold, his penis shrivelled, his scrotum tight, dark poison rich blotches sprawled over his stomach.

His lifeless eyes followed the route of his departed spirt, hushed out by one last deep breath, soaring into the sky on its path to the world where no one alive dared venture.

I kissed his cold lips, the blood on his lips dried. Slowly, with gentleness, I slid his lifeless head from my lap onto the earth.

I rose up, the bark grazing my back and buttocks.

A lonely owl howled a nocturnal cry, lamenting the departure of life, I wondered if all souls arrived at the same destination, who will hug the owl when its time has come, who will hug each animal when they die, mostly a violent death as nature devour its own.

I felt good being here for this departed soul.

A cry escaped from my mouth as the garrotte carved into my neck, the pain shooting down my limbs excruciating.

The stars dropped from the sky and exploded in my eye sockets. Above my head a tear spilled forth from a tragically sad butterfly face. It willed me to fold my wings and die with it a silent winter night sigh. Its whisper reached my ears, 'You are going to die,' the butterfly said to me.

No! No! No!

My fingers reached for my neck.

Taut cold guitar string cut into my hyoid bone. Salvador-Arana, I just knew.

With one finger under one coil, I pulled, the second coil tightened.

A double garrotte!

The ancient silent assassin weapon of choice.

My head yanked firmly in place against the tree.

I smelled him, my hands reached out behind my back, desperately trying to get hold of something, a leg, an arm, a genital, anything to release the strangulation, fighting the faintness in my head, willing the deoxygenated blood exiting from my brain, time was precious, I had four to five minutes maximum, spit drooled from my mouth.

I wriggled, increasing the pressure on my trachea, distorted visions projected on my eyelids.

I screamed as bark raked into the raw flesh of my index finger. I felt bruised, drugged by the pain. My mind screamed for consolation from the threatening death. Mother Abishag, please, help me. General Venter, come to my rescue. Lieutenant Herholdt. Please, anybody, someone, come to my aid and pull me from the jungle of death closing in on me. I knew not how much longer I could withstand the hostile action of the purple volcanoes. Black shadows moved forward with stealth. An overwhelming invasion of the tropical night. The great blackness threatening visionary abolishment

I slackened my body, forcing body and mind to succumb to the strangulation, relinquishing to the ultimate form of power and control, handing my life over, air control no longer mine, but his.

'Let go Socio,' Salvador-Arano murmured in my ear, 'you are careless my little desert rat, you cannot care for the soul once it's gone, dropping your guard, how fatal, handing your life on a plate to the ones lurking in the dark, waiting to take you from behind, taking your most precious possession, life. You let death come as a surprise to you.'

His lips caressed my ear, like a caring lover. His lips charged with such a feeling of anxiety as if he struggled with an internal prostration.

'Join me, I will teach you, train you in the beautiful art of assassination, the ancient traditions of honourable men who kill to survive, to control. You feel the fire, I want to burn with you, I want to fix your dreams, control the air you breath. The world order needs men like you. Succumb to me as though I am a god.'

The string loosened.

I gulped for air.

His warm hands closed tightly around my neck.

Two thumbs guarding cautiously over my windpipe, the slightest increase would crush my throat.

His fingers stroked the marking. His lips sealed mine. His body pressed close to mine.

I brutally gasped under the onslaught of his hard cock.

Sexual arousal welled up in me. I responded to his fond kisses of my neck and face. I smelled him as I snuggled in his arms. I ought to say, in that moment, I felt very drunk and completely knocked over.

Salvador-Arano pressed his lower body erotically, slowly gyrating, his fingers controlling the oxygen flow to my brain, giddiness, pleasure and fear fused, masturbatory sensations washing like a great tsunami down from my brain and up from my groin. He shivered and shuddered as we suck on each others lips. Our tongues hungry. All at one something so incredible happened, I wanted the moment never to end.

I started to groan, overwhelmed by powerful sensations, as erotic streams met somewhere in my abdominal region. Wave after wave of semen gushed out in a sudden and forceful steam, like poison spurting from the serpent fangs.

I gasped, the angel white light blinded me and my body released a warm jet stream into the cool night air. Stunned, I slumped as the hands dropped from my neck and he removed his hands from my body.

A sob brook loose, was it me or him?

I kicked the corpse stretched out in the grass away from me.

It rolled over twice. Its skull hit a large rock and cracked with a dull and heavy sound. The dead eyes of Julius gazed up at the Milky Way.

'Who are you? Why did you not kill me?' I ask of Salvador-Arano.

He looked at me and smile.

'I am just crazy, and crazy for you.'

'What do you mean,' I asked.

'This.' He indicated the semen dripping from my flat washboard stomach. 'This was not in my brief. I expected a fat hairy pig of an AfriKaner man. Not a young stud muffin of a, what is the word your cojones us for boys like you?'

'Cute?' I said.

'Don't you get cute with me. I may just turn you around and put my penis where it belongs.'

'Now where may that be,' I said, 'oh let me guess.'

He pulled me closer and sunk his tongue deep into my mouth. His Argentinian saliva tasted honey sweet.

I let him explored my sweet teenage mouth for a while, whilst caressing his ever so firm buttocks. I could not wait to get naked under cool sheets with him, then dive naked into a pool for a deep penetration session, then run naked into the sea and swim away with him to live forever as a mermaid in a land far-faraway.

Salvador-Arano let me go.

'Not bad, not bad, at all,' he said, wiping his mouth with a devilish naughty glint in his eyes. I pulled my hands back from behind his back. In an unguarded moment they fell down and roamed on their own accord around his crotch, as if aliens controlled them.

The devil of a hunk was hard. His big cock laid erected to the right. It got to me. I breathed harder.

'I want to make you come,' I said.

A low laugh escaped from his and his mock clasp his hand over his delectable seductive mouth.

'It can wait, something was worthwhile waiting. I want to take my time with you. We must get out of here, soon this forest will swarm with the enemy.'

Uneven early morning day light bursts burst into the dense vegetation mass of the  forest, signalling night-end to the sleepy lives buried in the undergrowth. The dark fringes commenced beating their retreat like soldier guards readying to return to their barracks. The air smelled warm and tropical. Somewhere a monkey called out in its sleep. The sky above the tree canopy now brilliantly coloured in an electric purple-gold hue. It was that most special golden moment of the day, the end of something and the beginning of another thing.

'Clean yourself,' he said, 'before the nocturnal creatures sniff you out and insist on making babies with you. I shall be too jealous.'

'Royal lovers are not entitled to jealousy.'

'Says who, Your Majesty, I am a man with a hunger. I traipsed this forest all night in search of my little queen.'

'Oh no suddenly I am reduced to a little queen, fancy that my lover with an international assassination reputation.'

'A tale for another day, let me have a look at finger

With a handful of leaves I wiped myself clean, the dizziness remaining, my throat tender and raw, as if I swallowed jewels of fire during barbaric ritual.

Salvador-Arano rubbed my asphyxiation spills into his T-shirt and jeans. Then, with a grimace, he tore the dead man's T-shirt into strips, tying the veins down with the precision and speed of a skilled orthopedic surgeon.

How long had I been haemorrhaging?

I sank down against the bark, but he pulled me up and dressed me in the jeans. This was all too-too a bit too much for a little sensitive thing like me. Perhaps I should reconsider my assassination career and insist on urban assignments only. I made a note to myself asking Captain Lisa Venter to arrange a whole day of spa treatments. Heavens know what irritations my delicate skin endured. I might be enflamed without being aware.

'Let's get you down the mountain, they will come for us once the old witch's trick wears off. You have been bleeding for too long, you need medical attention.'

Oh my, how butch my man sounds. My man! Oops, did I just think that. Little hussy I scolded myself. The apple fell not too far from the tree, like Mother, like son. What will Abel say when he hears me talking like this.

The night sounds returned to the forest.

The crickets resumed their night songs, wings fluttered high above the trees, nocturnal creatures departing on hunting flight paths, chasing, looking for life, movements to terminate in order to survive.

Little animals scuttered on the forest floor, trading one hiding place for another

'I warned him, warned him against you, he refused to listen. It could have been you.'

He pointed at Julius.

'I pitted two young bulls against each other, the strongest survived. Let me be your matador Kaner. I watched you closely. We want you to join us?'

'We?'

'The Brotherhood of Men, the Hashshashin.'

He stared intently in my eyes, reading me, scanning the hidden workings of my mind.

'I trust you, if not, well.'

He did not finish his sentence, but clasped his index finger and thumb around his Adams apple in a mock killing gesture.

'Join us, work for us, carry the tradition forward, honour the Hashshashin code, follow Asas, forget about Jesus, he was a lightweight, look, he ended on the cross, his enemies outclassed him. Forget about parliament politics, military politics, men in suits and uniforms, draping titles and medals around them like cheap jewellery dangling from a puta.'

He spat, a bitter twist drooping from his left mouth corner.

'Cojones without......'

His contempt so deep-felt, he could not finish his sentence, two tight fists rose up in the air in a men without balls gesture.

'Cowards,' he uttered at last, 'men using other men to fight their dirty battles. Old dogs without teeth, if an old dog is tired of fighting, he should retire to his corner and spend his life in the shade, keeping cool, not keep showing his worn out teeth.'

'You mean betray my country, how could I?'

'You betrayed your country a long time ago mi caro. You fight a one sided cause, it is wrong, you do not fight for your country, you fight for the cajones. You are their mask, you are guided by their false idealism. When they are done with you, they will toss you aside. This system you defend will come to an end, the forces out there in the world will withdraw support, will force the white government to its knees, for they want the monkeys to rule the jungle, its much easier to control the dark ones than the clever white ones.'

He kissed me on the lips.

'I am not like you, but I can liberate you from this trap you find yourself in. Come, do it, join us. Be strong, brave'

'Who are us?'

'The Brotherhood of Men. We are the silent voice of

the world. We carry our arguments out by other means. We hand peoples the power of self liberation. Our love for the human race guides us. We eradicate the weak and evil, we view the world as one, the defeat of one country is a defeat for humanity. There are no boundaries in the struggle to death our leader said, for many strong and famous men have guided us through the centuries. You cannot betray us, or the cause, you cannot escape us, no mind is higher than us, no king, no emperor, no president or premier has more power than the Brotherhood of Men. We eliminate and substitute those who fail our cause. Death is the ultimate penalty when the Brotherhood of Men is betrayed. We care for nothing else but the survival of the human species, not matter who you are. Will you join us, become an upholder of the human life?'

I nodded, enchanted, enthralled.

'Good, let's go back to City of Gold, life carries on, there is no respite, you lost a finger, a small price in poker game, I have drugs and thread in my car, I cater for human casualties, not flat tyres, let's get you stitched up.'

We started walking towards the forest. Soon it would be day light. Monday morning by my calculations, unless I'd lost more time than I care to remember. A new day would dawn.

As we stepped into the forest, I asked Salvador-Arano to walk on, he nodded, kept walking, I felt his trust, I gave him my word, the word of a man.

I turned around.

Leaves blew onto the black body.

His dreams ended, his aspirations now longer valid,

his reality living on in a world far beyond the edge of time, running wild in a world not known to us.

And I, where was I, what was to happen to me?

I was no longer a boy. The boy who walked on hot dusty roads had grown up.

I looked down at my feet and smiled, still bare feet, but no longer filled with dreams of flying away on a Hadida.

My story was not over, I would keep writing the chapters of my life, somebody out there was writing my story into their chapters.

Some with love, some with hate, but as long as humans take up the pen of life, writing chapters, life would continue, my life would continue, in their dreams, their fears, their desperation, this is life, nothing more, nothing less.

The fragments of my life, the fragments of their imaginations and contrariwise.

I shrugged my shoulders, it did not matter.

I was alive, I could see the moon-blue sky, the wind tops weaving in the night breeze, hear the leaves rustling, feel the bruises of the nights, I stroked the marks on my body, rubbing the blood clogged stub over my chest. Another mark on my left hand.

Would I be able to kill with my left hand?

The marks of a warrior. A warrior with a passion, a cause, a warrior following in the footstep of men who roamed this earth for centuries, guarding over humanity, protecting the finest species ever to have wandered this planet.

I squinted, a movement caught my eyes.

A little black spider sat poised on the firm, round

Zulu buttocks watching me with tiny black eyes.

I smiled at it, it raised a claw, the wind gently lifting its wispy grey hairs into the air.

I turned around and started to follow the broad back and wide shoulders of the Argentinian, who wandered into my wonderland 48 hours ago, in front of me.

I followed him with eyes opened wide, leaving my yesterday behind, the memories living on inside, but for now safely locked in the vaults, until such time as the need arose to revisit the of the past.

Time to report Operation Triangle Sun as completed in 50 hours.

*THE END*

Printed in Great Britain
by Amazon